WHO KILLED ZAIDA MOORE

WHO KILLED ZAIDA MOORE

D.E. JOYNER

Published by Alabaster Books
North Carolina

This is a work of fiction. Names, character, places, and incidents either are the product of the author's imagination or are used fictitiously and any resemblance to actual persons, businesses, events, or locales is coincidental.

Copyright 2006 by D.E. Joyner
All rights reserved. Printed in the United States of America. No part of this book may be reproduced in any manner whatsoever without written permission except in the case of brief quotations embodied in critical articles and reviews.

Published by Alabaster Books
P.O. Box 401
Kernersville, North Carolina 27285

Book and cover design by
D.L.Shaffer

First Edition

ISBN:09768108-9-1
Library of Congress Control Number:
200693506

10-06

To Brenda,
Thanks for all your love and support. You are, and always have been, "one of my own."
Enjoy W.K.L.M.
Slim

This book is dedicated to my two beloved daughters, Susan Miller and Cindy Pyburn.

ACKNOWLEDGEMENTS

My thanks to:
David Shaffer for his technical help. His beautiful cover design still leaves me breathless. John Staples for his careful and very thorough editing of my work. The writers group, Joanne, Lynette, Dixie, Larry, Helen, Dave, John, and Kathy. You were each so very helpful. Becky and Wade Swaim. You two have been more than just good friends. Thanks Becky, for your support.

1

Captain Jim Donavan headed down the hall past the radio room to the cafeteria to get a cup of coffee. A fifteen-year veteran, he was the officer in charge of communications for the Tampa Police Department. Three sergeants, six sworn personnel, and nine civilians completed his chain of command. The capable, well liked captain was not the most handsome man on the police force, but he had a bearing that commanded total respect from all who knew him. His six-foot-two inch frame carried his two hundred pounds well. His large hazel eyes were expressive in a square face. Exposure to the sun had caused a complexion that showed more wear than most thirty-eight-year old men.

"Wait a minute, he just walked through," said the radio operator on duty. "Captain this call is for you. It's a guy and he's very upset and crying."

The captain walked into the radio room and picked up the phone.

"Jim Donavan speaking. Who, who's this? Get a hold of yourself. I can't understand a word you're saying. Who? Bob Moore? Is this Bob Moore? You say Zaida's passed out on the floor and she's turning blue? Did you call 911? Cover her up, Bob, she could go into shock. I'm on my way.

Turning to the raido operator, Jim said, "Something has happened to Bob Moore's wife Zaida. I'm leaving now. Tell Inspector Burnette where I've gone. I'll be back as soon as I can find out something."

He turned on the siren and was at the at the Bayshore address in less than ten minutes. Bob was one of Jim's best friends, and he had been to the Moore residence many times.

As he pulled into the driveway, two paramedics were running for the front door. When Jim reached the door, he was met by a sobbing Bob Moore, who was totally out of control.

"I don't know, Jim, they've just started working on her. She's not responding. They both have worried looks and the lady paramedic is shaking her head. I don't know, but it looks bad," Bob cried.

Jim hugged his best friend around the shoulders. Taking his handkerchief from his back pocket, he shook it out, and handed it to Bob. "Let's see what's happening inside."

As they entered the double front doors, the first thing that Jim saw was Zaida lying in an almost prone position at the bottom of the stairs. Her coloring was truly a blue-gray. The two paramedics were compressing her heart and giving mouth-to-mouth resuscitation. Jim had seen a lot of dead people. Since becoming a police officer, he had spent much time in traffic, patrol and detective divisions. He knew the paramedic's efforts were futile. "Bob, let's go into the kitchen and get a drink of water. They have everything under control. If they need us, they'll let us know."

Bob was inconsolable as the two men stood beside the utility sink near the back of the kitchen. As Jim took a step backwards, he bumped into a basket of roses that protruded just slightly from the counter they were placed upon. One of the deep red roses had fallen onto the floor. Jim stooped to pick it up and put it back where it came from. He noticed that an arrangement of roses was incomplete. Some floral oasis was bare and a bow attached to a wire was lying on the counter. He looked at the unfinished bouquet and thought how living beauty and death's ugliness, so opposite an effect on the emotions, dwelt side-by-side in this unlikely environment at this time.

"Is she going to die, Jim? Is she going to die?" Bob asked as he cried uncontrollably.

Jim knew from past experience the depth of his friend's sorrow. He also knew he had to deliver an encouraging word in his time of need.

"Now let's not cross that bridge until we have to. It's really hard to cause a person's death. You know the will to live is strong, especially in someone so young."

"I don't know what happened. I found her on the floor when I came from the office. Please Lord, please Lord, don't let her die," cried an hysterical Bob Moore. He told Jim he had already called both their parents.

"Try to be strong Bob, Zaida will need you to be under control." As Jim tried to comfort his friend, the male paramedic entered the kitchen. His face was pained and drawn.

"Sir, we've done all we can. I'm afraid your wife is dead."

"Oh no. Why? How?" screamed a totally destroyed husband.

Jim knew he had to keep his composure. If his friend ever needed him, this was the time. Involuntarily, his eyes filled with tears. He brushed them away with his hand. He could barely utter a sound as he looked at the still, lifeless form on the floor. Finally, he found the voice that had temporarily deserted him.

"Bob, I'm staying with you until your family and Zaida's family can get here. Do you have a coverlet or sheet that we can put over Zaida?"

Bob left the room and returned with a pink throw. Bob and Jim each took the end corners and gently laid it over the corpse. Then they went into the family room to await the arrival of the families. Jim said to his best friend "Bob, you know anytime there's an unexplained death, the police will investigate. There are a few things they'll have to know."

Sobbing, Bob said, "They'll know one thing, Zaida fell down the stairs. That's evident."

"Now Bob, it doesn't work that way. The unexplained death offense report has many areas that must be filled in. That makes it completely uniform. Men in the patrol division, who first investigate, are well trained and have a procedure to follow."

"Jim, will you stay with me while the officer questions me?" Bob pleaded.

"No Bob, that's not possible. You know as a captain, I'm aware of the rules and regulations that apply, and I'm sworn to follow them."

"Jim, what are some of the questions they'll ask?"

"I really think you should wait for them to be asked before you become concerned," Jim advised his friend. "You won't need to pre-think the answers. They'll be immediate responses."

Bob repeated again, "Jim, I'm certain she fell down the stairs."

"She may have, but that will be determined after the investigation, you know an autopsy might be performed if the county coroner feels the need for one." Jim added.

"The thought makes me sick," Bob sobbed.

"One thing I do want to bring to your attention, Bob, is to be truthful in all questions asked, even the ones you don't see a need for. If you deviate one little bit from the truth, a cloud of doubt will hang over your entire testimony. You are dealing with men who are professionally trained in all areas of reporting unnatural deaths and the investigation of same. There's nothing left to guess work That's the reason it's called uniform crime reporting. I won't be present. They can handle this situation. The paramedics have already called them and they should arrive shortly."

The police arrived before the parents. Jim Donavan spoke to the young officer, excused himself and left the room. If needed, he would surely have offered his services, but the officer and the crime scene experts knew the exact procedures to use under the circumstances.

After quietly greeting the two sets of parents, Jim left the distraught family alone. On the way back to the station, a very upset James Palmer Donavan pulled into a drive-thru to get the coffee he had started out to get when this nightmare began at 1500 hours. It was now 1730 and he was emotionally drained. Placing the coffee in the holder, he pulled the patrol car under a giant oak, one of many that surrounded the perimeter of the parking lot. He completely lost control, pounded the steering wheel with both hands, he cried unashamedly as the past took control of him.

Jim Donavan and Bob Moore had been best friends since high school. They went to different junior highs that fed into Hillsborough High They were both on the football team and members of the National Honor Society. That was where the commonality ended.

Robert Earl Moore was the son of the owner of the largest electrical contracting and supply company in the area. The Moores were not always highly successful business people. Their fortune changed in the early 1940s. During the Second World War, Bob's grandfather, who owned a small electrical supply, repair, and contracting business, was lucky enough to bid on and win a huge government contract. He fulfilled all obligations and established an excellent record for future bids.

At the time of the Second World War, the Tampa Bay area was strategically important to the military. Two large bases were housed there. Also several small, but important training bases helped the war effort to succeed. Due to the needs of the military, a small family business, which furnished a comfortable, but not extravagant living, became one of great wealth.

The Moore's home was almost a three acre estate located on the Hillsborough River. The family preferred to live on that side of town since they had been residents there since nineteen twenty. The area where they lived was not only scenic, but furnished access to the Gulf. At the back of the property was a well-built dock jutting out into the river. Moored to the dock was a fifty-five foot yacht. Its every detail spelled luxury. The whole Moore clan spent entire weekends aboard it.

While well to do, the Moores never forgot their early struggle. They weren't social climbers as are many of the new rich. They were known for their contributions to the worthwhile needs of the community. Their support was always forthcoming when the need arose.

James Donavan's father was a bridge-tender. The need for this occupation isn't there today as much as it was three to four decades ago. The job, when needed, was a low-paying but stable income. The elder Donavan either couldn't or wouldn't seek a more lucrative position. His family never complained or made demands on their husband and father.

Jim's mother tried very hard to supplement the family's income by taking in sewing. She was good at her craft, but the demand and earnings were scant. When she had nothing on the cutting board or machine, she picked up alterations from the neighborhood dry cleaners. This was a pay by the piece deal and the cleaners had to have a cut, which left almost nothing for his mom. Her philosophy was that anything beats nothing, so she kept on keeping on, adding a little contribution to the family's survival.

Their home in the Seminole Heights area was neat and well cared for. The boys made certain that the yard was beautifully maintained. Though not elegant, the house furnished a comfortable home for the family. There were always good meals, well prepared and well served. Many times extra faces could be counted at the large dining table. The Donavan's home, although not filled with priceless antiques or fancy bric-a-brac, was always filled with love.

It was not possible for Jim to go to college. When he graduated from high school, he took a job with the local newspaper. His job entailed delivery of morning papers to substations. Home delivery people picked them up, as did numerous businesses such as restaurants, grocery stores, etc. The pay wasn't fantastic, but Jim learned the valuable art of getting along with people. Even without college, he did okay. When Jim turned twenty-one, he took the civil service exam for a police officer position at the Tampa Police Department. He passed the test with flying colors, and after excellent training, became a sworn police officer..

At the age of twenty-three, Jim married a young lady he had met soon after becoming a policeman. They had a brief courtship, and after their wedding, settled into a small but comfortable home.

Before long, Dot and Jim were expecting their first child. When James Palmer Donavan, Jr., was born, Bob was honored to be named the baby's godfather.

On the other hand, Robert Earl Moore attended Georgia Tech. He received a degree in electrical engineering and went to work in the family's business. In his mid-twenties he married Zaida Spencer, a beautiful local socialite. His life included country club membership and one showplace of a home in one of the most exclusive and historic sections of the city.

Even though Bob Moore and Jim Donavan's lives were on different tracks, they remained best friends. They met for lunch often and were always available to discuss even the smallest problems.

Bob was aware of the social needs in the area, and when Jim mentioned that a certain police sponsored activity had a financial need, he came forward without prodding and answered the call.

2

Chief John Fallon, Deputy Chiefs Roger Bain, Jerry Smith, Inspectors Bridges, Garcia and Burnette held a closed door meeting the day after the death of Zaida Moore. No interruptions was the order given the chief's secretary. The meeting was held to discuss the death of the wife of one of Tampa's leading citizen's, under unusual circumstances. The crime scene investigators had done their job. The patrol division had completed, approved, and referred the original report to the detective division, and the coroner's office, as was the procedure for all unnatural and unexplained deaths.

Chief Fallon spoke. "Sometimes it's necessary to withhold information from the press or other citizens, who would have access to copies, unless it was considered confidential."

Inspector Burnette asked, "How long do you think this report should be considered confidential?"

The chief's reply was, "We'll keep it confidential until we have a suspect in custody. Then, we'll determine if the time is right for a press release."

Inspector Bridges inquired, "Chief, what if someone questions if the Moores are being given preferential treatment because of who they are."

"That could and might happen. Our stock answer will be that we are protecting the victim's rights and the integrity of the investigation. That should satisfy anyone's curiosity."

Deputy Chief Bain brought up a point not mentioned. "Chief, I marked my calendar that you would be attending 'The chiefs of police conference for the entire week starting Monday morning. Normally, I am the acting chief in your absence. Will that be in effect, and if so, do you want me to make decisions concerning the confidentiality of the Moore report?"

"Yes, as usual, you will make any and all pertinent decisions," the chief replied.

"Chief, you know there is a night-beat news reporter who continually gives our people a hard time. He questions almost every report and demands copies before the offenses are even numbered. I think he's an EMT and fire truck chaser. Will you address this, please," Inspector Burnette asked.

"If he gives them a hard time about the Zaida Moore report, tell them to tell him I said I would personally call his boss and have him transferred to classified," the chief threatened.

That brought a chuckle from the inspectors and deputy chiefs seated around the table. They all knew the reporter without his name being given.

Deputy Chief Jerome Smith brought up a question. "Chief, how long will it take for the autopsy to be performed, and are we the only ones who will receive the results.?"

"Jerry, as a rule, it's completed in about three days, and it is a public record.. If something irregular is discovered during the procedure, further tests may be required. Usually the doctor will call us and explain the reason for the delay. Hopefully, the death was caused by an accidental fall down a flight of stairs, and not by a perpetrator. Are there any other questions that need to be addressed before we adjourn?"

Who Killed Zaida Moore?

Each man gave a negative sign or answer. The chief said, "If you think of anything, you can call me on my private line and we'll discuss it. I'll make sure that each of you know the question and answer."

Every one got up and left the chief's office and went to their assigned position. They felt totally empowered in the joint decision made concerning the confidentiality of the Zaida Moore offense report.

The coroner carefully read the report and immediately ordered an autopsy. He was in no way impressed with the social status of the victim, or the fact that the family was known for its generosity with the police department's needs. The attending pathologist was Dr. Kenneth W. Sheppard.

Chief Fallon sent a memo out to all divisions that no information of any kind would be forthcoming on the Moore offense. Also, no reports or supplements were to be given to the newspaper reporter assigned to the Tampa Police Department.

Foul play was not suspected, but the report was sent to the detective division with homicide detective Moe Garrett assigned. Garrett wasn't your run of the mill detective. He had means and ways of investigating a murder that other officers wouldn't think of.

To give a valid description of Moe Garrett would not be possible since men and women would probably see him in a different light.

A woman would see him as a sharp dresser, absolutely sexy in personal appearance. His slightly graying hair called attention to his expressive, deep blue eyes. A good straight nose and full lips accented a deeply clefted chin. All of his features went together perfectly.

D.E.Joyner

A man would see Moe Garrett as a good guy, easy to talk to, someone who worked out and had a good build and who was generally neat. Both men and women would surely admire his walk. He walked with a determination.

Moe had been on the police force for almost eight years. He had put time in the traffic division and did well. His knowledge and ability on a Harley-Davidson made the job a snap for him. Not only was he good at the basic level, but he had the ability to deliver a very distressful and sad, but necessary message, to loved ones whose kin were involved in fatal accidents. He had a way of saying what had to be said with tender compassion. This made accepting the terrible news a little less traumatic.

After traffic, he was assigned to the patrol division for two years. He often said he had originated more juvenile runaway reports than any other five officers combined. He always knew when report cards were due to go home. He would have at least five kids who couldn't face their parents with the results. Usually, these turned out fine with written reports cancelled, sometimes even before the offense was turned in to his sergeant. Sometimes he told the runaway, "If you were mine, I'd spank you."

Of course there was sadness in patrol as they investigated the deaths of children. Moe had a thing about babies choking. He had written one report of a little one in a playpen choking on a small piece of grass that came through the slats. "After it happens, all the precaution in the world can't change it," he would say regretfully.

As a detective, Moe Garrett was without equal. The thing that earned him respect from his peers was his police savvy. He was street smart, with ways and means to get things done that some officers never even dreamed of. The saying around the department was, "If Moe Garrett couldn't solve a case, you'd better inactivate it, or put it into a file that didn't demand immediate, constant attention."

He had snitches lined up to give him information. If they were in a tight spot financially, Moe would dig deep to let them have money. He took them out to eat at good restaurants. He was not ashamed to be seen with them. He was an all around good guy, a lawman for all seasons.

3

About Moe Garrett

Moe was born in a small town in South Georgia. His family was poor but hard working and strived to get ahead. In the early fifties, his father was offered an opportunity to move to the Tampa Bay area to work at a local shipyard as a welder. He was such a good employee that his company increased his wages rapidly. Because of this, he and his wife were able to purchase a nice home for their growing family which included an infant girl and two school aged boys.

Both boys were good students, Boy Scouts, and both played little league baseball. It was about this time that Moe was given the nickname that would stay with him.

He loved the game of baseball and put forth more effort than almost any other member of the team. He played catcher, which demanded that he watch intently the entire playing field. When he could make a play at home plate, the coach would yell, "Throw the ball to Morris." Soon, to be more time efficient, he started to cut the order down to "Throw the ball to Moe." The name stuck and soon all his buddies started to call him "Moe." Then, everyone started to call him Moe. Everyone, that is, except for his mother. She refused, saying that she named her son Morris, not Moe, one of the Three Stooges.

Who Killed Zaida Moore?

As Moe matured, he displayed leadership qualities. He was outstanding in R.O.T.C. when in high school and seriously considered a career in the military. At about this time, the war in Viet Nam worsened, and he decided to put college on hold and use his R.O.T.C. training to serve his country. He joined the Army just before his nineteenth birthday. After intensive training, he was accepted as a member of the U.S. Army Special Forces.

Before he left for Viet Nam, at the age of just under twenty, he married his high school sweetheart, Stacey Smith. They were a happy young couple with hopes and dreams for the future. Stacey took a job at the telephone company. Her attractive good looks and intelligence helped her get interviews for promotions. It wasn't long before she was in an excellent position.

Moe made rank quickly due to his aptitude for the military and his leadership qualities. He didn't enjoy being away from his bride, but he knew the time would pass quickly and he'd soon be home. Their letters were frequent and filled with love.

Stacey had acquired a management promotion which placed her in a position working closely with a young engineer. As so often happens at the workplace, they soon saw one another from a different perspective. She was giddy and attentive when they were alone. Before long, the working relationship had become a sexual one.

Over in Viet Nam, Moe thought all was well, and he counted the days until his time would be up. He diligently saved his money to buy their home as soon as he could get back.

One day when he was on a photo-taking detail, he saw a small boy, alone, in an area laced with land mines. Without thinking, Moe jumped from the Jeep and grabbed the child. He was almost back to the road when he stepped on a mine. His leg was badly injured, but he held onto the child until help could arrive. Even though his injuries were severe, his leg was saved by a determined doctor. He had huge scars on his legs and shrapnel in his ankle. For his bravery, Sergeant Garrett received the Bronze Star. The fact that he had to go home early didn't bother him. He felt that he had given enough of himself for his country.

As a surprise for Stacey, he decided that he wouldn't let her know he was coming home. When he was in California, he bought her a beautiful soft green negligee. He could hardly wait to see her in it.

Moe called her from the Tampa International Airport. Stacey answered the phone with a chill in her voice. She said she was sorry but she couldn't pick him up. Her car had been giving her trouble and she was afraid to make the long drive. Needless to say Moe was terribly disappointed, but understood. His loving parents happily picked him up and dropped him off at his apartment.

When Stacy opened the door, she had a 'cat that ate the canary' look on her face. She gave him a friendly kiss and said that he looked well under the circumstances.

Moe knew immediately that something was not right. He thought perhaps his wife might be a little shy. After all, they had been separated for over a year. They had little to say to each other and seemed like strangers.

"Moe, I need to tell you something. There's no need to put it off any longer. I'm in love with someone else. I've been seeing him for over six months. Please believe me, it's nothing you've done. I never planned for it to happen this way." This true confession, delivered by his supposedly adoring wife, caught him by surprise.

Moe was speechless. He just looked at her with tear-filled eyes. What he did next defies reason, except the heart of a twenty-one-year old was broken beyond repair. He grabbed the box containing the negligee, placed it on the floor and stomped it repeatedly and screamed. He then pulled the garment from the box and tried to rip it apart. Screaming and cursing, he rushed from the apartment and called his mother to come get him.

For six weeks he stayed drunk. He didn't want to see anyone, not even family members. He was still obligated to serve nine more months in the army. Due to the his leg injury, he checked in regularly at the local V.A. hospital. He was honorably discharged a little early. While entitled to a disability, he didn't claim it. His leg injury did cause a slight limp which he worked hard to overcome. To some (especially women) his walk was sexy. He felt that it left him slightly impaired, but he didn't dwell on it. It never kept him from passing a physical exam.

Time began to heal both physical and emotional wounds. When Moe had regained his perspective, with the help of counseling, he decided to take advantage of his G.I. benefits. He enrolled at the University of South Florida. He hadn't made a decision on what he wanted to do with his future, so he started with the basics. He did know one thing though, he wanted no part of a career in the military. His maturity was intact, therefore college was successful. He graduated magna cum laude with a degree in criminal justice. The Tampa Police Department had openings for bright, ambitious young men interested in a career in law enforcement and Morris Daniel Garrett filled the bill.

While Moe was being counseled, he met a graduate student whom he found interesting and exciting. They shared many of the same ideas and enjoyed one another's company. They were married one week after he was sworn in as a Tampa police officer. He joked that the only reason he married Lou Ann was to have somone to wake him up in time to make role call at the police department. The truth of the matter was they were a young couple very much in love.

4

The autopsy report arrived on the third day after the death of Zaida Moore, the day before the funeral was scheduled. Detective Garrett read the report carefully: 'The body is that of a well developed Caucasian female thirty-two years of age. Weight 130 pounds, height 5' 7". The cause of death was blunt force trauma to the back of the head. The fatal wound is three centimeters by six centimeters. It is the opinion of the attending pathologist that the lethal blow to the autonomic nervous system shut down the autonomic responses such as breathing (respiration) and circulation causing immediate death. No sign of life was observed by the attending paramedics. It is the opinion of the undersigned pathologist that the death of Zaida Moore was not the result of a fall down well carpeted stairs'.

Kenneth W. Sheppard MD Pathologist

Coroner's Office County of Hillsborough, State of Florida.

Detective Garrett read and reread the report. His only comment, said to no one in particular was, "Well I'll be. My work is cut out for me." He pulled a small notebook from his coat pocket and copied names from the offense report. Any person at the Moore's residence on the day of her death was listed. The number one person on the list was the victim's husband, one Robert Earl Moore.

Her funeral was an elegant affair. Grief screamed from each person present without one sound being made. The eulogy offered by Zaida and Bob's minister focused on her many acts of kindness and generosity. She was portrayed as a consumate lover of her fellow man. Roses, her favorite flowers, were placed in every window in the sanctuary.

Detective Garrett made a cursory appearance at Zaida's funeral. He tried to be as inconspicuous as possible. His presence was to observe the behavior of the grieving widower, his parents and Zaida's family. Also, he looked for signs of another woman's attention to the bereaved. Nothing really jumped out at him, and his empathy was evident and intact.

As Captain James Donavan, who was a pallbearer, walked down the aisle, he acknowledged Moe with a slight nod of the head. At no time was one word exchanged by the police officers.

Mr. Moore was interviewed at the Detective Division the second day after the funeral. The interview was held in a small, private conference room. A table and four upholstered chairs took up most of the area. There was a sideboard which held a Mr. Coffee Machine. A small sugar bowl and creamer filled with Coffee Mate packets was beside the coffee maker. A pitcher filled with ice water was available. Plastic and thermal cups were stacked beside the ice water. Spoons, stirrers, and napkins were boxed on the sideboard. A small wastebasket sat on the floor nearby. The room and its furnishings could only be described as austere.

The interview went as follows. "Mr. Moore, be assured there are no listening devices, two way mirrors, cameras or other means of recording or preserving this interview. I will, however, be taking notes to supplement the original report. You are free to talk without jeopardy. Be truthful in all questions and answers. I realize that you've been under tremendous strain and it's not my intention to cause you further stress. Do you understand?"

"Yes sir, I do," answered Bob Moore with a voice showing a slight bit of nervousness.

"Please state your full name and date of birth."

"My name is Robert Earl Moore, my date of birth is June 9, 1955."

"Where do you reside?" Detective Garrett asked.

"I live at 2824 Bayshore Boulevard."

"How long have you lived at that address?"

Bob thought aloud, "We moved in about Christmas 1984."

"Does anyone else live at 2824 Bayshore Boulevard?"

"Not really, but we have a guest cottage in the back. At this time, it's being occupied by Zaida's sorority sister from college and her friend from Nashville."

"Is her friend male or female?"

"Male", Bob answered, he's a stock broker and real estate investor. Look, Detective Garrett, I don't condone what they're doing, but really it's none of my business."

"What are their names?"

"Her name is Susan Parker, and his is Mark Pierce."

"I'll probably talk to them soon," an interested Moe replied.

Now Mr. Moore, I want you to tell me exactly what happened on the day your wife died."

"I came home around two o'clock. I didn't see Zaida, but her roses were on the utility sink. I thought she was in her office using the phone. I opened the fridge and took out a soda.

I walked into the family room and saw Zaida's feet and legs at the bottom of the stairs."

At this time, Bob Moore began sobbing. Detective Garrett stopped the interview and total silence filled the room.

"Can we go on?" he asked after about five minutes.

"I'm sorry."

"I understand," Moe said as he stood and walked to the watercooler. He filled a paper cup and handed it to the distraught husband. "Now when did you call 911?"

"I'm not sure, but I think it was about two-thirty."

"Did you attempt to resuscitate your wife?"

"I did. She made one small sound and that was all."

"What did you do then?"

"I called Jim Donavan. He's my best friend. I thought he could offer some help."

"What time did you call him?"

"I think about two-forty-five."

"How long have you and Zaida Moore been married?"

"We were married June 5, 1982."

"Okay now, would you call your marriage a happy one?"

"That depends on how you define happy. We didn't argue and fight if that's what you have in mind. I was very generous with my wife and she with me."

"Mr. Moore, is there anything about your relationship that I need to know?"

An agitated Bob Moore responded, "May I ask exactly where you're going with this line of questioning?"

"All right, let me put it another way. Could someone other than you have been in love with your wife?"

Mr. Moore answered strongly and quickly, "Positively not. We were totally devoted to one another."

"Did your wife have any addictions or medical prescription needs?"

"She hardly took an aspirin, but I'll have to admit Zaida did, in fact, have a little drinking problem. I wouldn't say it was severe, but she drank more than the wine that doctors recommend for heart health."

"Are you saying that your wife did have a drinking problem?"

"You might say so."

"Mr. Moore, can you think of any reason why someone would want your wife dead?"

"Absolutely not. Zaida was loved by all who knew her."

"Did you kill your wife?" the detective asked. He knew what the answer would be, but he wanted to observe the response to the question.

"I did not." an emphatic Bob Moore answered.

Detective Garrett got up, put his notebook into his coat pocket, and walked Bob Moore to the door. "Thank you for your cooperation and may I say as a husband and family man, you have my total sympathy."

Bob Moore and Moe Garrett shook hands and Moore closed the door behind himself.

Moe took out the small notebook that he had just put into his pocket, opened it, and wrote beside the interview notes. It is my opinion, and it's subject to change as we get into the investigation, Bob Moore in no way fits the description of a wife killer. Check 911 to check on time call was received.

5

Moe didn't think the housekeeper was so grief-stricken that she wouldn't be able to talk to him.. He knew she worked the day before Mrs. Moore died. That information was given by Susan Parker, the guest of Zaida, to the officer who investigated the death . Garrett had found that housekeepers are frequently told things by the lady of the house that no one else knows. He hoped Jean Hodges, the name given by Susan on the offense report, would be able to shed some light on the events that happened the day of the death.

    Moe had no trouble locating the address of Jean Hodges. Her name and address was in the rotary file from the time she was a complainant in a bicycle theft. He recognized the address as being in one the local housing projects.

    The next morning found him pulling into the entrance of the local housing project, as it is called by those living there. Built in the late 1930s, it has always been well maintained. The yards were kept neat, mowed regularly, and the parking lots were free of debris. They don't allow vehicles parked for days that didn't run.. Public housing wasn't the Taj Mahal, but this project furnished a dwelling place for over eight hundred residents. The tenants were generally low income or were on welfare. They were thankful to have a roof over their heads.

As Garrett slowed the unmarked police car, heads could be seen in most of the windows. They breathed a sigh of relief when he parked in front of No. 422, Court B. Even though the car was unmarked, some of the residents could smell Tampa Police Department all over it.

Detective Garrett got out of the car, observed everything around him and walked toward the door. Before he had a chance to knock, a tall, heavy set woman about thirty appeared. She was not unattractive, but surely not someone who demanded a second look. She had the aura of one who worked hard and spent little on self-improvement.

"Are you Jean Hodges?" Moe Garrett asked.

"I am. Tell me who you are and what you want."

"Did you know that one of the people you clean for had died?"

"I didn't know it 'cause I don't take the paper. I found out when I went out Monday to clean."

"Who told you?"

"You know they have a guest house in back. There's a Miss Parker staying there now. When I got to the house, she met me and told me about the death and the funeral held the day before. She said that Mr. Moore would let me know when to come back. I had a key to the back door and she asked me for it."

"Mind if I come in, I want to ask you a few questions."

"Sure, come on in, but you'll have to excuse the house. I'm so busy cleaning for other people, I got no time to clean my own. You can sit on the couch, but be careful. Sit between the cushions or the springs will stick you."

"I won't keep you long. It's important that I talk to you."

"I'll do anything I can to help. I been working for Mrs. Moore for over three years, and she's been fair with me."

"You say you've worked for her for over three years?"

"Yes sir," Jean Hodges answered the detective. "I go there every Monday and Thursday. I get there about 7:30 a.m. and usually leave around twelve-thirty. Mrs. Moore always fixes me a sandwich because the transit bus takes an hour or more to get me home."

"No car?" Detective Garrett frowned.

"I'm hoping to get me one in less than a month. I'm getting a tax refund any day now, and it'll more than make the down payment."

"Mrs. Hodges, are you married?"

"I was," she acknowledged, "but I got a divorce over a year ago. He's in jail now for selling drugs, right here in this project. Now don't get any ideas, I don't use drugs. I've never used drugs. I have an eight-year-old son and I'd never do that in front of him."

"Your ex the boy's father?"

"No, I'm not sure about his real father. I was seeing two men when I got pregnant."

"Tell me, was there anything unusual when you went to clean the Moore's house last Thursday?"

"No, not really. It was a little messier than it is sometimes. I thought maybe the Moores and Miss Parker and Mr. Pierce had had a party."

"You mean the people in the guest house?"

"Exactly."

"Do you know them well?"

"No, not really. I kinda know her 'cause she's been there before. I don't know him at all, but Mrs. Moore said they were from Nashville."

"Tell me. Was Mrs. Moore drinking last Thursday?" Moe still wondered if perhaps Zaida did fall down the stairs.

"Detective, did you say your name was "Grimes?""

"No, I said Garrett, Moe Garrett."

"I have a rule that I always follow: What I hear there, what I see there, what they do there, stays there. Do you understand?"

"Yes, I understand and I agree with you completely, but we are talking about murder. The coroner's office returned the results of the autopsy and he said she did not die from a fall down the stairs. Moe said nothing about the murder weapon or cause of death being a blow to the back of the head."

Jean Hodges was silent. She avoided making eye contact and twisted her hands.

"Well?" he asked.

"All right, I have to tell you something. Mrs. Moore wasn't herself last Thursday. She was even mean to me. I was dusting the banister and she pushed me away when she was coming down the stairs."

"Did she use force when she pushed you?"

"Aw, the push didn't matter. It would take somebody bigger than Mrs. Moore to move me. What she said did. She called me a snaggletooth, low-rent bitch and said that the law ought to take Jason, my little boy, away from me and put him in a decent home. Jason is the most important thing in my life and I'm doing all I can for him. You see, I'm a third generation in this housing project. I want to do better for him."

Detective Garrett looked at the cinder block walls, old and barely basic light fixtures, worn out, chipped, asphalt-tile floor covering and pitiful furniture. He felt depressed just looking around, and he knew how hurtful Mrs. Moore's remarks must have been.

"Did you say anything to defend yourself?" Moe asked.

"No, my mother always said that drink takes away your reason. I needed the Moore job bad."

"You didn't say one word?"

"No, I knew I could take her, but if I hit her, I'd wind up in jail and then what would happen to Jason?"

"Mrs. Hodges, are you sure you didn't hit Mrs. Moore?"

"No. I wanted to hit her bad, but I couldn't take the chance of hitting her and losing my job. The two days I work for Mrs. Moore pays my bills. If I could pick up another day during the week, it's spending money for Jason and me."

"Did you say Mrs. Moore was drinking?"

"Well yes, it seemed like her drinking was getting worse. I never used to see Mrs. Moore when she was tipsy. For about a year now, I've not seen her when she wasn't. Sometimes she would lay on the couch and go to sleep. When she got up, she would be kinda shaky and wobbly. One day when Mr. Moore was home he told her in front of me that he didn't want another drop of whiskey in the house. He said he was tired of smelling perfume mixed with Scotch.

I felt real bad for her when she told me that she had lost a little boy. She said she was six months pregnant and already had the nursery ready for him. Sometimes when those diaper commercials come on, she had a sad smile. She said Mr. Moore thought she should get on with her life, but she just couldn't do it. I don't think Mr. Moore really had much feeling for her. It seemed that his business was the only thing that mattered."

"One last time, you didn't hit Mrs. Moore, maybe with the iron or something, did you?"

"I did not hit Mrs. Moore with anything, period. Yes, I wanted to, but I didn't."

"You know that you may be asked to take a polygraph exam. I'll be in touch with you. Thanks for the information you have provided."

As Detective Garrett left Jean Hodges' apartment heading back to his car, he had to step over and weave in and out around a multitude of tricycles, plastic cars, tractors and various other riding toys. No doubt bills went unpaid so loving parents could provide their tots with something that made both lives more enjoyable.

Moe Garrett, the father, thought about the grand lifestyle the Moores lived. He knew, if given the same set of circumstances that Jean Hodges had experienced, he would certainly have wanted to pop Zaida Moore just once.

It was true. Public housing furnished homes for those in need, but it was not always the perfect setting. As Garrett left the area, he looked back and shook his head.

When he walked into the Detective Division, he was met by Inspector Bridges. "Well, Moe, did you find out anything from Zaida Moore's cleaning lady?"

"I'm putting it in a supplement boss, but I can tell you this much, Zaida Moore was no Mother Teresa."

6

You could set your watch at 0745 each morning as Robert Gonzalez walked through the door at the back of the records section . Robert was a pillar of strength to everyone who knew him. He managed over forty women of all ages. Keeping that many females happy was at times an awesome responsibility.

The first thing Robert did when he arrived was to check the duty roster to determine who would be working at a certain position on a given day. He realized that certain personalities clashed and did his best to make sure he kept those apart. After the duty roster, he went to the rotary file. He could tell how much work had been done by the number of complaint and defendant cards filed. He knew his people were on the ball if every card had been filed. Sometimes, regardless of how hard they worked, it was impossible to get all the work done. He was always very conscious of the entire staff he supervised, and gave the benefit of the doubt if not sure of their effort.

Robert surveyed the entire section before he went to his desk to begin his day. He studied the offense reports and the traffic accident reports. At close to 0800 hours, he would go to the desk where everyone signed in. Pen in hand, he waited until the minute hand on the office clock was exactly between the one and two on twelve. He then drew a line under the last name on the sign in sheet. Anyone signing below the line was late, regardless of the amount of time or the reason. The kind boss was indeed a stickler for promptness.

When he was seated at his desk, his day had begun. He never stopped working and was available to help each one and answer a multitude of questions.

Robert was numbering the offense reports when he was interrupted by Betty Simpson who was copying the traffic accident reports for distribution. "Mr. Gonzalez, there's a man at the counter who would like to speak to you."

"Did he say what it concerned?"

"No, he just asked to speak to you."

Robert brushed his hands and got up from his desk chair and headed to the counter where a man was waiting. "What can I do for you, sir?"

"I hope you can help me. I'm Charles W. Wilson, private investigator. I have been retained by Mr. Preston Spencer; the father of Zaida Moore, to further investigate the murder of his daughter."

"I wish I could help you, but the report is confidential and no one may see it but the detective assigned to the case and two other police personnel. I can copy the front of the offense report for you, but that's all. Any other information will have to come through the chief's office."

"Is it possible to speak to the chief?"

"I don't know his schedule, but he often speaks to citizens who make a request. What did you say your name is?"

"Charles W. Wilson, licensed private investigator, here is my identification," the man said as he pulled out and opened his license case and showed it to Mr. Gonzalez.

Who Killed Zaida Moore?

Mr. Gonzalez walked over to his desk and picked up the phone. He pushed the button to the chief's office and straightened some papaers while waiting for an answer.

"Hello Ann, fine and you? That's great. Did your boss leave for his convention yet? Say he's meeting with the deputy chiefs and inspectors? What does his schedule look like today? Nothing at ten? Would it be possible for you to ask him if he would speak to a Mr. Charles W. Wilson at that time? Why don't you write it on a piece of paper and put it before him. I don't think he would mind, do you?"

Ann wrote a sentence on a piece of paper and put it in front of the chief. He didn't speak, but nodded his head in the affirmative. Ann returned to the phone and informed Robert that the chief could see Mr. Wilson at 1000 hours in his office.

Robert returned to the counter where Mr. Wilson stood with his fingers tapping a rhythm on the gray formica countertop. He obviously expected a negative answer and had a rather cross expression on his face.

"You're in luck, my friend," Mr. Gonzalez said totally disarming the private investigator. "The chief will see you at ten o'clock. That's an hour from now. Why don't you go around to the cafeteria. It's open to the public and the coffee isn't bad."

Charles Wilson thanked Mr. Gonzalez and leisurely walked around the hall to the cafeteria. He enjoyed the coffee and observed the happenings around him.

At exactly 0955 Mr. Wilson walked through the door to the chief's suite. Ann greeted him and invited him to have a seat in one of the two chairs available. "Sir, what is your name?" Ann asked as if she were filling out a questionnaire.

"I'm Charles W. Wilson, a Florida licensed private investigator," he responded as he removed a business card and handed it to her.

Ann pushed the inter office button and announced, "Chief, Mr. Wilson is here."

"Send him in."

Chief Fallon stood and shook hands with Charles Wilson. "I'm glad to meet you. I'm John Fallon."

"I'm Charles Wilson, Chief, and I'm glad to meet you."

"Exactly what do you wish to speak to me about?" inquired the chief.

"Sir, I'm a Florida licensed private investigator. I have been retained by Mr. Preston Spencer to further investigate the murder of his daughter, Zaida Moore."

"Our department has an ongoing investigation with an excellent homicide detective Moe Garrett, leading the team of investigators."

"My services were requested by Mr. Spencer over a week ago. I had never met him, but I did surveillance work in a domestic case for one of his clients. He was pleased with the results and mentioned me to Mr. Spencer. You can understand their devastation at their daughter's death."

"You know we have the report marked confidential. I don't feel we can compromise the investigation by letting anyone, I mean anyone, have access to it."

"Is that your final answer, Chief?"

"I'm afraid so. Don't think we're down on private investigators. We're not. As a matter of fact, several have helped us tremendously in the past. You may have copies of the original report. I know there's not much information on it, but times and dates are vitally important. Tell Mr. Gonzalez to make you two copies. By the way, where are you from?"

"I'm originally from Jacksonville. I've been here almost six months. Thanks very much for your help."

Wilson left the chief's office and headed to the records section. The chief closed the door and picked up his private phone, dialed an extention, and spoke briefly. Within five minutes Moe Garrett was standing beside Ann waiting for the chief to invite him into his office.

"Moe, come in please."

"Chief, Inspector Bridges said you wanted to see me."

"Yes Moe. A private investigator has been hired by Zaida Moore's father, Preston Spencer. Is there a reason why he would think he needed additional help with the murder investigation of his daughter?"

"No Sir. We're moving along, and have had several interviews. No one stands out as a prime suspect yet. You know it has only been ten days. What do they expect? Chief, I understand how they feel, but I think they're clutching at straws."

"That may be the case. Now, here's what I want you to do. Find out everything you can about Charles W. Wilson. He's a private investigator from Jacksonville, Duval County. I could do it myself, but I think it would set off an alarm. You never know to whom you're speaking."

"Chief, Charles Wilson is probably a common name in Jacksonville. Can you give me a physical description?"

"Let me call Ann. She can help with this. Ann, please come into my office."

"Yes, Chief." Ann stopped what she was doing and entered the chief's office.

"You spoke with Charles Wilson the private investigator that just left. Will you give Moe a physical description of him."

Moe had his pen and pad ready to take notes. "I'm ready, Ann."

"I'd say he is thirty five years old, more or less, six feet tall, weighs one eighty, a lot of dark brown hair, brown eyes, medium complexion, no scars or tattoos visible. Oh yes, he had a deep dimple on his left, no, right cheek." Ann said.

"I'll tell you one thing, you really looked at him, didn't you?"

"Moe, you know I appreciate a good looking man. That's why I like you so much."

"Don't 'BS' me Ann. Is there anything else you can add?"

"He had long, thick eyelashes," Ann gushed just before she made a grrr sound.

"Now Ann," the chief joked, get a hold of yourself. We don't want to see you brought up on a sexual harassment charge."

Ann left the office and both men shook their heads. "Moe, she's the most efficient woman I ever knew and she has a sense of humor. I wouldn't trade her for a pot of gold. Now, the business at hand. When you find out about Ann's sexpot, let me know."

Moe left the office and went back to the detective division. He called the Jacksonville Police Department first. He identified himself and asked to speak to someone in the criminal investigation unit. He was speaking to Captain Byron Lindsay almost instantly. He told the captain his name and reason for his call. He was very careful not to leave the impression that the police department didn't appreciate a private investigator horning in on their territory. He gave the captain the name and was told that he would get back to him with the information.

"I'll give you my number if you'd like. It'll save you some time," Moe answered.

"I think I have the information available," the captain thanked Moe.

Moe knew the reason for the captain's callback.. He wanted to be certain the person to whom he spoke was indeed a police officer. He wanted the record check to go through the proper channels. Moe had taken fewer than five breaths when the phone rang. He answered with his name and title. Captain

Who Killed Zaida Moore?

Byron Lindsay was calling from the Jacksonville Police Department.

"Captain, we spoke a few minutes ago concerning a private investigator working for a client in the Tampa Bay Area. Oh yes, I do have that," Moe responded to the caller's request for the person's name. "I don't have a date of birth. I have a physical description. I'll wait. Let me know when you're ready," Moe said as the captain expressed the need for the proper form for the record check. When Garrett gave the description, he kept it strictly physical.

"I'll fax you a photo of a man I think fit's the description Call me back when you receive it. Here's my private number."

Moe had the photo in a few seconds. He took it to Ann and asked if that was the man who was in her office earlier.

"That's him," she ascertained.

Moe returned to the privacy of the detective division and called Captain Lindsay. When he answered the phone, Moe confirmed the identity of Charles W. Wilson. The information from Captain Lindsay was as follows: "Charles Westley Wilson was a member of the Jacksonville Police Department for three years. He voluntarily resigned, reason not given. He then went to a position as security for a large grocery chain in the Jacksonville area. The reason for his leaving that position was personal injury in the line of duty."

As a policeman, Moe was interested in the personal injury. "Sir, is it possible for you to divulge the type of injury?"

"Yes, Detective, the injury is a public record. There are no restraints on it. This is what happened. One night Wilson was working security at a grocery store. A cashier alerted him a customer had shoplifted groceries. When he approached him, the shoplifter bolted for the door. Naturally, Wilson chased him out and into the parking lot. When he finally managed to catch him, the two men grappled and the shoplifter wrested his gun from him. He fired at Wilson and the bullet struck him in the lower abdomen. It deflected and struck him in the genital area and lodged in the upper thigh. He hovered near death for over a week, and was forced to wear a brace on the leg for months. Naturally, he had to resign his position.

As the culprit ran away, the stolen items slipped from his tucked in shirt. Basically, Wilson got shot over two cans of Vienna sausage and a box of saltines. The shooter threw the gun down, but it was impossible to lift prints from it as his hands were sweaty causing the prints to smudge. He's never been apprehended."

Since Wilson was a former police officer, Captain Lindsay was familiar with the shooting and the reason Wilson resigned from the police department, but privacy laws prohibited divulging any of that information. He didn't make any further comment except to say Charles W. Wilson had taken a fingerprinting course to enhance his job possibilities. He ended the conversation with a wish that the subject do well in his new endeavor.

Moe had a lot to tell when he started his conference with the chief. He listened to Moe's account of his conversation with the captain. When Moe was finished he said, "You don't have anything to worry about. He's not going to hamper the investigation. He probably can't tell a whorl from a tented arch."

7

Moe left the chief's office and headed straight to communications. He wanted to check with Captain Jim Donavan to see if he knew Zaida's father had hired a private investigator to look into the murder Even though no arrest had been made yet, he was just a little surprised with the announcement. He knew the detective division was working several different angles in the investigation.

He entered Jim's office and sat down. He knew the captain wasn't far away as his cigar was still smoldering in his desk ashtray.

"Moe, did you know that Zaida's father has hired a private investigator to work on the murder?"

Moe answered, "Jim, I just found out about an hour ago one has been hired. The chief called me in and told me. I assured him we are diligently working on the case. The private investigator is a former police officer. He resigned and had taken a job with a large grocery chain in security. While apprehending a shoplifter, he was shot and permanently disabled. He has a Florida license and is originally from Jacksonville.

The reason I was aware of Preston Spencer retaining him was a telephone call I received from Bob Moore last night.

He said Preston Spencer thought a different approach might be effective in solving the murder.

"Jim, you know we've been trying to put together the total picture, but a piece of the puzzle is missing. Usually, when a murder is committed, we arrest the killer quickly or we put the word on the street that we need a little help. It never fails, a snitch comes from nowhere with valuable information. We have run into a dead end in the Moore case. There was no evidence of a struggle, no indication of a vendetta, nothing in her life sent up a red flag. She apparently was a well adjusted, wealthy, beautiful young socialite with everything to live for. I understand the Spencer's feelings. They are so saddened by the murder. In a sense, you might say they subconsciously want revenge."

Captain Donavan responded. "What you've said is true, and I'd probably feel the same way if it were my child. Moe, I know you interviewed Bob. How did you feel after the interview?"

"Yeah, I interviewed him day before yesterday. I don't think he was involved in any way. I'll say one thing, if he was, he's one hell of an actor. I've never seen a man so broken up."

"You know I've known Bob for years, and he's one of the nicest, kindest people I've ever met. I wouldn't think him capable of murder, especially Zaida's. Those two were inseparable."

"I'm going to talk to the gardener soon. Maybe he saw something or someone that will shed some light on the investigation," Moe said.

"When I was talking to Bob, he said he thought some of Zaida's jewelry was missing. He couldn't be sure, but two pieces on the insurance schedule are worth more than twenty thousand dollars. They are not in her jewelry box. I realize the house was in a state of chaos the day of Zaida's death, but I'm a little suspicious of Mark Pierce who's staying in the guest house. I know Bob said he was a stock broker and real estate investor, but he could be a jewel thief from Los Angeles. You know Nashville is the perfect place for him to operate. Those country music stars are replete with expensive jewelry Now I could be wrong. There are many Mark Pierces on file."

"Jim, I'll go this morning to talk to Mark Pierce." Moe said.

"When you get his complete name, date of birth, and last known address, call me with the info. By the time you get back here, I'll have it all put together for you. I think this may be a lead. You know with our new technology, we can run a records check on him in less than a minute. I can even get a photograph. It's not like it used to be when we had to depend on other department's interest to get the info back to us."

Detective Garrett thanked his friend for his help, shook his hand and left the cigar smell behind.

The ride out Bayshore Boulevard was always an uplifting experience. The double drive was centered with a beautifully landscaped median. Built in the early 1900s and maintained well, it was located on the Hillsborough Bay. Many residents who lived on the south side of Tampa used the Boulevard for their daily commute to downtown. The traffic was generally heavy and fast moving. The Bayshore, with its wide sidewalk on the bayside was perfect for jogging and strolling babies. The several miles long Bayshore Boulevard is one of the country's most beautiful drives.

The building lots on Bayshore have always been high dollar. If one were available today, it would probably cost at least a million dollars. In the past, old mansions were set far back on large lots. They were beautiful, but no longer desirable, and have been replaced with lovely modern homes occupied by the very wealthy. The Moore's home was no exception.

It was built in the 1980s. The two story French Country Style was over five thousand square feet of living area. The lower level was gray brick, with the second story stucco painted cream. The house trim was rust.

The porch ran completely across the front of the house. It was twelve feet wide. Three arches with stucco finishes were across the front. The center one was large to accentuate the double doors which were painted grey with rust trim. The brass door handles and hinges were magnificent. The other two arches were smaller and decorative. Windows were set back into them.

The porch roof was, no doubt, internally supported by an "I" beam that rested on six, eight inch in diameter gray Italian marble columns. The floor of the porch was dressed in foot wide marble squares that matched the columns.

The balcony had a three foot high railing that was very tailored in stucco painted cream. The balcony floor was rust tile. A long marble table, gray in color, rested on a metal base that matched eight metal chairs.

An interesting accessory was a beautiful sixty inch wide white marble sideboard. It had two doors, each of which had a circle on the inside. If you pressed them, a refrigerator was exposed. The top, which was forty-eight inches high was a convenient serving area or a perfect spot for a floral arrangement.

The bay was beautiful, especially at night, and the balcony was the perfect place to view it in peace and privacy.

A wide red brick walk stretched from the drive to the center of the porch. Marble steps with a brass railing completed the ensemble to this most luxurious home.

A long brick drive to the house was bordered on either side by a ten foot wide rose garden. It ran the length of the drive, ending when it approached a three car garage. On the far side of the garage end attached was a storage shed used by the gardener. At the back left, was a small garage apartment. It was

Who Killed Zaida Moore?

the same color and style as the house. The size was not impressive, but it was very attractive. The garage under the apartment was accessed by the same brick drive that enters the garage.

Detective Garrett parked the unmarked car on the driveway and walked upstairs to the entrance of the dwelling. A solid brass door knocker was set in the middle of the heavy, ornate wooden door. Moe struck the knocker twice and stepped back. His wait wasn't more than ten seconds when a crack appeared at the door. He could see feminine features in the opening.

"Yes," came a sexy voice from the inside.

"Mam, are you the houseguest?"

"Yes, I'm Susan Parker, Zaida Moore's best friend."

"Is there a Mister Mark Pierce also here?"

"He's in the shower. Who did you say you are?"

"I'm Detective Moe Garrett from the Tampa Police Department. I need to speak with Mr. Pierce."

"Come in and have a seat, I'll tell him you're here."

"Thanks," he said as he walked into a beautiful sitting room. Everything was so perfectly arranged that it encouraged the eyes to search further. Moe didn't think he had ever been in a more elegant or beautiful environment.

Within five minutes, his concentration was interrupted by someone walking near him. The gentleman who came into the room was surrounded by a good masculine smelling shaving lotion. He was wearing a short maroon robe over what appeared to be blue silk boxer shorts. He could have been described as movie star handsome.

Detective Garrett stood, "I'm Moe Garrett from the Tampa Police Department. Are you Mark Pierce?"

"I am," he responded.

"I'm here to ask you a few questions about your activities on the day that Zaida Moore was murdered."

The robe clad, handsome man settled into a loveseat. He patted it beside him and motioned Susan Parker to sit. When she sat, he pulled her close and patted her arm. He seemed to be aware of her grief over the untimely death of her best friend. As he spoke, it was evident that he was somewhat stressed out at the events of the past two weeks.

"Detective, we think that Zaida may have fallen down the stairs. I spoke with her earlier and she had been drinking. She was taking some Easter decorations upstairs to the attic. Some of those things were clumsy, but she could go up with them okay. We feel she may have slipped coming back down the steps."

"Your theory sounds credible, but according to the autopsy, the fatal trauma was caused by an almost square object. He determined that the injury, where it was on the lower back of the head, could not have been caused by a tumbling fall."

"Well, unless you witness such an accident, it's really hard to tell how the body might shift during the fall," added Mark.

"You could be correct, but in cases such as this, the experience of the pathologist always comes into play. We consider him the authority and last word. Let's get on with our interview."

"What is your full name?" Detective Garrett inquired.

"My name is Mark David Pierce."

"What is your date of birth?"

"I was born on 26 April 1958."

"Place of birth please?" asked Detective Garrett as he took notes in a small notebook.

Mark Pierce answered, "I was born in Los Angeles and lived there until about two years ago."

"What is your current occupation?"

Who Killed Zaida Moore?

"I'm a stockbroker and real estate investor. My business is in Nashville."

Detective Garrett had all the information he needed and immediately asked if he might use the restroom. "I'm sorry, but a couple of my detective friends and I went to breakfast, and I must have drunk four cups of coffee."

"Sure," Susan got up and led him down the hall to the bathroom.

With the door shut and locked, Moe took out his cell phone and dialed Captain Donavan's number.

"Captain Donavan here."

"Captain, Moe Garrett."

"Moe, I thought you would never call. Got the info we need?"

"Yes, Mark David Pierce, DOB 26 April 58. Born and raised in the Los Angeles area, lived there until two years ago. I'll see you later. Wait for me to come in."

"Great job Moe, I'll see you in my office."

As Moe returned to the sitting room, he breathed a sigh of relief to reinforce his need for the restroom. "Can we continue our interview?"

"I'm at your command, Detective Garrett," Mark Pierce said with a much too accommodating voice.

Moe had him pegged as a "yes man" who really knew how to work a room. "What were you two doing on the day Mrs. Moore died?"

"Susan and I went out to lunch at 12:10 p.m. We ate at a restaurant on Bayshore. We've been there before with Zaida and Bob. Oh yes. One thing I just thought of, I went out earlier in the day to buy some ribbon for Zaida. She had drunk a couple of cocktails and she made a practice of never driving with even one drop of alcohol in her system. I didn't go into the house when I brought the ribbon back. She met me at the back door and took the ribbon and her change."

"Did you see anything unusual before you left or after you came back from lunch?"

Susan shook her head, and Mark answered, "No, as we left, the gardener was talking to Zaida. He had cut a basket of roses and was carrying it in as they walked to the back door."

"Mark, you and Susan know that anyone present on the day of the murder may be requested to take a polygraph exam. It may inconvenience you, but don't leave town unless you call me or have heard from me."

"Bring it on, I've got nothing to hide."

"Thanks, both of you, for your help. I'll be in touch."

As Detective Garrett left the apartment, he felt two pairs of eyes follow him down and out to his car. He couldn't wait to talk to Jim Donavan and lost no time getting back to the police department.

Moe parked his car close to the back door which is normally used by the building engineers and prisoners called trusties who clean the jail, took out the garbage, and occasionally did requested favors for uniformed personnel. As he turned the corner and headed to the radio room, he spotted Captain Donavan, hands on his hips, cigar in his mouth, and a serious expression on his face. Removing the cigar, the captain almost yelled, "What took you so long?"

"I didn't waste any time, Jim. The traffic was heavy. It was bumper to bumper on Bayshore."

"Sorry Moe, I didn't even think about that. Come on into my office, this is strictly confidential."

Moe sat down and pushed his chair back as far as he could to get away from the smelly cigar. He almost felt like praying that the Captain would get himself one of those personal air purifiers to put on his desk."

Who Killed Zaida Moore?

"Moe, listen carefully to what I'm telling you," the former detective said "You gave me all the info I needed to find out about Mark David Pierce. He's no more a damned stock broker than I'm a member of the U. S. Supreme Court. He's a known jewel thief who served eighteen months of a three-year sentence in a California state prison. There are no active wants or warrants on him now, but once a jewel thief has perfected the art, they rarely give it up. The Moores are people of means who have spent a fortune on jewelry. Their residence, with his free reign, is made to order."

Detective Garrett couldn't believe what he was hearing, but he knew that this information would mean at least one more trip out Bayshore. "No shit, Jim," was all he could say.

"Keep this information to yourself. You know if Pierce found out about our knowledge, he'd leave the state. I doubt if we could get him back if we needed him. You know Moe, it's kind of sad. Most jewel thieves are usually bright, good looking, charming people, attributes that would insure success in many fields, but they use these assets to lure unsuspecting victims like the Moores."

"Thanks, Captain. I can't believe that Susan Parker has been duped by this imposter."

"Moe, you should know by now that some women can't resist a handsome man anymore than some men can't resist a sexy woman."

"I'll say this, Susan Parker is one sexy woman."

"Maybe they deserve one another. Is she married, Moe?"

"I really don't know, but I'll get the scoop when I go back there in a few days."

Not another word was mentioned about the Moore case. When the two officers entered the cafeteria, they discussed an upcoming deep sea fishing trip planned by the Fraternal Order of Police for all uniformed personnel.

8

The private investigator had little to go on in solving the murder of Zaida Moore. He had the approximate time of the offense and the address of the victim. Little else was furnished by the police department. Charles (Chuck) Wilson had to rely on his years as a police officer and his mature thinking.

The day after he was retained, he put everything into motion. Chuck Wilson decided to do a little neighborhood snooping. He had to depend on a city map since he wasn't familiar with the south side of town. He found the Hillsborough Bay and the drive Bayshore Boulevard. He checked the numbers and found the one he was looking for. He turned right at the next intersection and counted three houses on the next street over. He couldn't believe the difference in the two areas. The street had homes that were nice, but certainly not pretentious. He pulled into the driveway he thought corresponded to the Moore house. He got out of the car, observed the surroundings and walked down a sidewalk approaching the house. Three brick steps put him on a stoop at the front door. He rang the doorbell and an elderly lady answered the door. She didn't open the door, but spoke to Chuck through the screen.

"Mam, I'm Charles W. Wilson, a private investigator doing some follow-up work on the Zaida Moore murder. I've been retained by Mr. Preston Spencer. Here is my identification. I'd appreciate a little of your time."

"Come in. I wondered why someone didn't come here to talk with me."

Chuck entered a foyer and turned right to go into a living room. Even though it appeared to be dated, it displayed elegance and good taste. He was quick to ask, "With whom am I speaking?"

"I'm Estelle Knight. I've lived here in this same house for forty years. My three children grew up here. I'm a widow now. I lost my husband last year. He struggled with lung cancer for eighteen months."

"Tell me Mrs. Knight, did you know the Moores well?"

"I guess I did. My daughter and Zaida were both cheerleaders at Plant High School. The Spencers didn't live close by. They lived in the Beach Park area. My daughter Pamela feted a bridal luncheon for Zaida when she became engaged. When she and her husband bought the lot in back of me, I was so happy for the young couple."

"Did you ever see anything that would cause you to think Zaida might be in danger?"

"No, not in a physical danger, but I did see things certain to cause trouble in her marriage."

Chuck's ears perked up and he quietly responded to the comment. "Do you mind telling me exactly what you mean?"

"Mr. Wilson, I'm not a nosy neighbor, so help me. This is what I saw. I was upstairs in my guest room getting ready for a weekend houseguest. I walked over to open a window and thought I saw movement on the Moore's patio. I took a second look and couldn't believe my eyes. Zaida and a strange man were cuddled up on an air mattress. I couldn't see exactly what they were doing, but I can tell you it was not something I would discuss with a stranger. Zaida got up and fastened her bikini top. He picked up the air mattress and let the air out as they walked arm and arm to his car.

"Do you know what kind of car it was?"

"I'm not sure, but it could have been a Mercedes, you know one of those little ones."

"What color was it?"

"It was silver with a black top."

"Now don't you think it strange that the twosome would cavort in such a manner when they could be seen from the surrounding areas?" Chuck inquired.

"You couldn't see from the ground level. The Moores have a seven foot cement wall surrounding their entire backyard."

"Now Mrs. Knight, is it possible you could have been mistaken about the person's identity? How far can you see accurately?"

"Is the moon 240,000 miles away?"

Wilson was engrossed in his note taking. When Mrs. Knight answered him, he shook with laughter. He thought she is one smart senior citizen. He considered her comments credible.

"Mrs. Knight, anything you told me will be kept in the strictest confidence."

"Mr. Wilson, now you would have thought they'd go into the house with the hanky-panky, wouldn't you?"

"Yes, you're right, but we never know what make people do the things they do, when they do them. I guess they had to seize the moment."

When Chuck turned onto Bayshore, he had to turn right as there was no access street in the opposite direction. He drove several blocks before he could make a left turn. As he passed the Moore house, he decided to stop and hopefully speak to someone. He had to turn around to be going in the right direction. When he pulled onto the brick driveway, he was impressed with the total beauty of the estate.

As he reached the end of the drive, the door started to rise under the guest apartment. A man in a Jeep stationwagon stopped when he saw the car and driver.

"Can I help you with something?" Mark Pierce asked.

"I'm Charles Wilson, a private investigator retained by Mr. Preston Spencer, Zaida Moore's father. Are you a resident of this home?"

"No, not a resident. I'm a houseguest."

"Will you speak with me, please?"

"I don't have much time, but I'll answer a few questions when I've seen some identification."

Charles Wilson pulled the badge holder from his pocket and handed it to Mark. "This enough? I'm licensed in Florida, formerly a Duval County resident."

Mark got out of his car and leaned up against the door. Charles propped his foot on the front bumper and Mark also took a stance there. "Did you know Mr. Spencer had retained private help with the murder investigation?"

"No, but I'm not surprised. It seems the police are dragging their feet."

The former policeman seemed to take issue with the comment. "I wouldn't say that. You know it's hard to tie all the lose ends together in just ten days. I think the Spencers are brokenhearted with their loss. Naturally they want to see more action. I understand how they feel."

"Did you have something specific you wanted to talk to me about?" Mark inquired.

"Did you see anything unusual on the day Mrs. Moore was murdered?"

"No, I can tell you she was fine around lunch time. She was talking to the gardener when my friend and I went to lunch."

"Now Mark, a confidential informant has said Zaida was having an extramarital affair. Can you elaborate on this statement?"

Mark paused as if he were mulling the question over in his head. "You know, it really doesn't matter now, does it? Zaida is dead and who cares anyway? Yes, Zaida was having an affair. It had gotten serious enough they were talking about leaving their mates and being together."

"Are you saying he was married too?"

"Yes, he and Zaida had dated in high school. They went their separate ways when they went to college. He is a C.P.A. in the downtown area."

Chuck could just imagine he had killed Zaida because she was putting the pressure on him to leave his wife. "You know what kind of car he drives?"

"Yes, it's a silver Mercedes convertible with a black top."

Bingo, Mark thought. Two people couldn't be wrong. "Now Mark, you know anything you tell me will be kept confidential. Can you give me the name of the man?"

"His name is Christopher Branch. His company is Christopher Branch and Associates. I don't know the location of his office, but I'm sure you can find it in the yellow pages under Certified Public Accountants. Charles, I've always thought being a PI would be exciting."

"Sometimes, but mostly I've worked domestic cases trying to catch wayward spouses in the act. I can't count the pictures I've taken of them going arm in arm into a 'hot pillow' motel. That's usually the event putting an end to the marriage vows. Can you think of anything else that would help the investigation?"

"No, nothing I can think of now, but if you leave a business card and I think of something, I'll call," Mark answered.

"Here's my card. I have my phone with me at all times."

Who Killed Zaida Moore?

Charles Wilson thought of going downtown to interview Christopher Branch, but decided to turn in for the day and evaluate the information he had collected. His day had proven to be most successful, and he anticipated the meeting with the two-timing C.P.A.

Wilson always kept a log of the day's activities. He wrote the following: *I was retained yesterday by a Mr. Preston Spencer. His daughter was murdered, and he wants me to further the investigation. I went to the police department this morning, met with the chief, who gave me the front (only) of the murder report. He seemed helpful, but was adamant in his refusal to lift the confidentiality order placed on the offense report. Interviewed a neighbor of the Moores. She knew Zaida, and stated she was having an affair. Mark Pierce confirmed her suspicion. Gave name of lover.* He initialed the log, as always, with CWW

D.E. Joyner

9

Chuck Wilson was up before the sun. He looked at the bedside clock which read 6:23 a.m. It's too early to get up Wilson thought, but he dragged himself up and into the shower.

    When he arrived in Tampa, he rented a condo off Dale Mabry Highway. It was centrally located with excellent traffic patterns on the main thoroughfares. He bought a minimum of needed household items and furniture. Some he purchased from the local Goodwill store. He knew he would eventually go back to Duval County for two reasons. He had a seven year old son that he missed terribly. Also, Duval County was home. He was born there and had never lived anywhere else.

    Dressing for the day, he chose a pair of tailored slacks and a muted plaid sport jacket. A mock turtle black pullover completed his attire. He looked sporty, but casual and professional.

    When he arrived at the neighborhood diner, he took a stool at the counter. As he was seated, the waiter served him a cup of coffee with a rich awakening aroma. He ordered his usual breakfast. As he ate, he glanced at the local newspaper bought at the entry to the diner. When he finished breakfast, it was time to head downtown where he planned to speak to Christopher Branch at his office in a local bank building.

Who Killed Zaida Moore?

There were many vacant parking spaces on the street, but he decided to park in a lot since he didn't know how long, if granted, the interview would take.

Wilson entered the building and walked to the directory beside the elevator. He found Christopher Branch and Associates located on the twelfth floor. He got into the elevator along with several other people. When it stopped on the twelfth floor, he got off along with several other riders. He stopped and looked both ways for a door number or a plaque that announced the company.

As he approached the door, he couldn't help but feel a little apprehensive. He had always thought C.P.A's. were rather quiet people, loners who were rather boring. He certainly never thought of one that led a double life which included a lover.

Wilson opened the door into a lovely office with a high ceiling area where huge plants reached for the sun coming through a stories high sunroof. Directly in front of the door, at her desk, sat an attractively dressed young lady keying information into a computer.

"May I help you Sir?" She asked.

"I'm Charles W. Wilson. Private investigator. Here's my license," he responded as he handed her his leather license folder. "If possible, I would like to speak to Mr. Christopher Branch."

"He just came in. Let me see if he can see you."

Wilson heard a man's voice say, "Yes, show him in, please."

"Mr. Wilson, Mr Branch will speak with you. Follow me, please."

Chuck followed the lady into a beautiful office where one of the men he'd seen on the elevator was seated behind his desk. "Thanks for seeing me. I'm private investigator Charles Wilson. I've been retained by Mr. Preston Spencer whose daughter Zaida Ellen Spencer Moore was murdered almost two weeks ago."

"I'm Christopher Branch, and I don't quite understand why you're here. I know nothing about a murder, and I don't know Zaida Ellen Moore."

"Mr Branch, I've had confidential information that you did know Zaida Moore. Her father feels that the police are dragging their feet in the investigation. I won't comment on that, but I will say they are nearly torn apart by the entire situation."

"Mr Wilson, I believe you and I are about the same age. We grew up in a society that still frowned on infidelity. Am I right?"

"I would agree with that statement. However, different circumstances can create different results. Right?"

Wilson could see Branch was having an inner struggle as to what would transpire next. "Very true. What proof do I have that you won't divulge information that could greatly damage my personal and professional life?"

"I can give you my assurance that I won't tell anyone about our meeting. If you are hiding something that's unlawful or criminal, then I'll have to expose it to the proper authorities. Even then, I'll tell you up front, the matter is out of my hands. Do you agree with this?"

"Mr Wilson, I trust you. You do appear to be a man of honor. I'll grant you the interview." Chris got up, shook hands with Wilson and shut and locked the door.

"Whatever I ask, please don't be offended. I don't mean to embarrass you."

Chris Branch's response was, "I understand."
"Before we start, please call me Chuck and I'll call you Chris, okay?"

"That's what I've always been called."

Chuck fumbled for his notebook as he searched his pocket for a pen. "Chris, did you know the victim Zaida Ellen Spencer Moore?"

"Yes I knew the victim."

"Was she a friend?"

"Yes, you could say she was a little more than a friend."

"Would you elaborate on that comment, please."

"It will take me a while, but I'll try to be thorough with what I'm going to say. Zaida and I were high school sweethearts. We started to date as sophomores. By the time we were juniors, our relationship was a beautiful love affair. I was her first love, and she mine."

Chris Branch was silent for a minute. His face was red and then a ghostly white. He tried to control a voice that was guttural, and then stifled deep sobs. The scene totally surprised Chuck who was speechless. Finally, he said, "Chris, just a minute. Can I get you a drink of water?"

"Please, if you don't mind."

Chuck walked to the water fountain he had noticed when he entered the office, and filled a cup with water. He handed it to Chris and patted him on the shoulder. "If you can't go on, I'll understand."

"You don't know how I've suffered since this tragedy happened. I couldn't grieve at home or here. It has been horrible. I couldn't even attend her funeral.

Chuck, we dated exclusively for three years and planned to marry after college. Zaida wasn't just beautiful, she was kind and caring in all areas of our life together. Even though she was an only child, she never showed a self centered personality.

When we went away to college, our parents decided we should sever our relationship until we were older. I know their intentions were good, but they failed to realize the depth of our love. Zaida went to a small college in Tennessee, and I attended the University of Florida. For a while, we called each other often, then we gradually drifted apart. Finally, we started to date others. I didn't marry until I was somewhat established in my profession. Zaida became engaged to Bob Moore before she graduated. When they were married, it really tore me up, but what could I say?"

"Have you and Zaida been intimate recently?"

"Not just recently. We met at a mall about three years ago. Zaida had just lost her first baby. She was upset and when I offered her my condolences, I hugged her. I don't want to sound sophmorish, but I was so excited I couldn't hide it. She, too, was affected. We planned a rendevous at their beach apartment. Since then, we've met at different places."

"You do have a wife, don't you?"

"Yes, I have a wonderful wife, but I've never stopped loving Zaida. You do understand, don't you?"

"Yes, that can, and often does happen. In my experience as a private investigator, I see more bad marriages than good ones. I've had a bad one. Now, do you have an idea who might have murdered Zaida?"

"No, I've thought about who could be responsible for this senseless crime."

"Did you and Zaida plan to divorce your mates and be together?"

"We talked very seriously about that move, but decided tearing up two families was just not the right thing to do. I have three children under seven years of age. My wife and I have often discussed her childhood and how her parent's divorce devastated her. We've agreed never to do that to our children."

"Chris, what were you doing the day Zaida was killed?"

"I was here at the office. I didn't take a lunch hour that day because one of my associates was resigning and we had a farewell lunch catered in."

Chuck asked, "Which catering service do you use?"

"We have one here on the ground floor in this building. It's called Food For All Reasons," Chris responded.

Chuck made a mental note to stop on the way out to check with the caterer.

"What did your wife do that day, if you can remember?"

"My wife volunteers at my son's school. He is in kindergarten. She reads stories to the class and takes them to lunch to give the teacher a break."

"Is there anything I should know you haven't told me?"

"I can't think of anything. You know, I feel better just being able to talk to someone about Zaida."

"I'll meet with Mr. Spencer. I see no need to relate one word of what we've discussed. Don't you feel they would be hurt to think they were responsible for you two kids not being together when the love was obviously so strong. Also, older people are not so accepting of infidelity. You can never tell, they might turn it around and blame you for their daughter's unhappiness."

"I appreciate you coming, and I'm sorry I couldn't contain my emotions any better. Leave one of your cards and if I need a PI, I'll call you."

"Thanks so much. I'm new here and need all the help I can get. Don't get up. I'll let myself out."

Chuck headed to lunch. He felt Branch was a good man and not involved with the murder in any way. He had a good, air tight alibi, and so did his wife.

As he was leaving the building he checked the directory for the caterer. He opened the door and entered a small office. He could hear cooking sounds coming from the back room. He rapped on the door and a lady wearing an apron came into the office. "May I help you?"

"Yes, a little information would be appreciated."

"Go ahead, but make it snappy. We have a luncheon in exactly thirty minutess."

"Did you cater a lunch for the C.P.A. Christopher Branch two weeks ago?"

"We did. He's a good customer. We served ten associates lunch. I think it was a retirement party."

With lunch over, Chuck arrived home and sat down at the computer to enter the day's activities. He couldn't help but reflect on his own life and its complications. His day was only half over so he decided to call Preston Spencer to see if they could meet in the afternoon. His secretary said he would be available at three o'clock. That gave him over an hour to wait so he needed to fill in some time. There were a few places he planned to see. Going toward town, he had seen a classic building with several minarets on top. He pulled into a side street and strolled around a beautiful park. He read a sign that identified the park as Henry B. Plant Park. He knew the name and associated it with philanthropy. He determined to come back to visit the museum when he had more time. He looked at his watch and knew twenty minutes could be spent in a traffic jam, if only a little fender bender occurred.

Preston Spencer, a lawyer, had an office not too far from the park, so Chuck had plenty of time to parallel park and walk to the entrance of the office building.

When he entered the lawyer's office, the entire scene reminded him of "To Kill a Mocking Bird." The furniture was old, the accessories were old, and the secretary was old. She greeted Chuck with a toothy smile that caused wrinkles to form around her whole face, even her forehead. When she called his name, Mr. Spencer came into the waiting room to invite him into his office. Chuck hadn't seen the office before, as their first meeting was at a restaurant in a local motel. He felt he was back in time about fifty years.

"Have a seat Mr. Wilson."

"Thank you, Sir," Chuck responded as he took a seat close to and facing the attorney's desk. "Your office is really unique."

"Yes, I've been here for thirty-seven years. It really hasn't changed much in that time. The practice of law has changed though. I was a go-getter in my younger days. Now I do a few wills, real estate closings, and advise clients about law suits they are considering. I've thought about retiring, but what would I do? I don't play golf, I'm not really crazy about traveling, and I don't have a hobby. I would be miserable, especially now that our daughter is no longer with us."

"Mr Spencer, I want to bring you up to date on my investigation thus far. I have interviewed several people including friends and neighbors. I don't think I could put a finger on a suspect now. The ones I've spoken to are all heartbroken about her tragic death. They had nothing to add to my report. All were so distraught."

"I know. Zaida was loved by all who knew her. She was precious, a real joy all her life. Her mother is in a state of deep grief. I don't know if she can pull out of it."

"I know exactly how you feel."

"Mr Wilson, did you know Bob Moore's best friend is a police captain?"

"Please call me Chuck. Yes I know that. I don't think it would compromise the investigation. I understand the detective handling the case is excellent."

"Oh, I don't doubt that one iota, Chuck. As a matter of fact, I think it's a plus."

"Well, I'll be in touch with you almost daily. If you need me for anything, you know how to reach me."

"Chuck, before you leave, I want you to meet my right hand. This is Mrs. Mildred Troxley. She came aboard less than a year after I started my law practice. We have truly grown old together."

"It's a pleasure Chuck. Speak for yourself Mr. Spencer. I'm just a little more mature than thirty-six years ago." Mrs. Troxley admitted.

As Chuck walked out the door, he could feel the stress the Spencers were under. He vowed to remove some of it, if possible, by finding out who killed their reason for living."

Log:
Today I interviewed Chris Branch, a nice C.P.A. He admitted his affair and love for Zaida Moore. Met with Preston Spencer, Zaida's father. Was introduced to his secretary, a Mrs. Mildred Troxley. A productive day.
CWW

10

Chuck was mulling over all the interviews he'd done and the various personalities he'd met. He was impressed with the genuine kindness of Mr. Robert Gonzalez. He thought about his meeting with the chief of police. He was dignity and authority personified. Preston Spencer was a perfect gentleman from the old school. He couldn't shake the compassion he felt for Chris Branch. What a situation in which to be enmeshed. As he thought of Chris Branch, he also thought about his unsuspecting wife, who knew nothing of her husband's double life. Or did she know? Chuck hadn't given much thought to her being involved. He knew many husbands had been slain by jealous wives who could foresee the end of their marriage. Chuck had determined to leave no stone unturned in solving the Moore murder.

He didn't have a city directory or crisscross to find out where Chris Branch lived, so he got into his car and headed to the city library. As he entered, he was impressed with the beautiful building and more impressed when someone offered to help him as he walked into the lobby. He was directed to the second story where all city directories were located.

City directories are like cemeteries. When you start looking at tombstones, one leads to another. It's also easy to get lost in an old city directory, especially one from over a hundred years ago. Chuck finally controlled himself and pulled out the one that was a year old. It didn't take him long to find Christopher Branch, C.P.A., his address and telephone number. He copied the information and walked to the help center. He gave the clerk the address and asked him if he could give him the name of the elementary school serving the area. He hoped Chris's child wouldn't be attending a private kindergarten.

The clerk knew the exact school serving the address and wrote the name and address of the school under it. "New folks in town?" he asked.

With tongue in cheek, Chuck said, "We're relocating from Jacksonville. We've found a house we really like, but the school is so important."

"Oh you'll love the school. The teachers are excellent and the parents are so helpful and supportive."

The clerk was so high on the school, Chuck was impressed even before he saw it. "Thank you for your valuable information," he said earnestly.

He went to his car and opened his city map to locate the school's street, and then drove there. The street was a four lane road with little traffic. He slowed down at the entrance to the school. The building, probably thirty years old, was a beautiful red brick with outside corridors. The visitor's parking area was well marked with three vistor spaces available. After parking, Chuck headed to the school entrance. There was something about entering a school that always excited Chuck. The office was to the right of the doorway. He coud see a lady sitting at a counter thumbing through a book.

"May I help you, Sir?" she asked.

"Yes, I think so," Chuck said as he took out his badge and business card.

"Are you the police?" she asked.

"No, I'm a private investigator. I need a little information."

"I'll help if I can."

"I just need to know if an specific person volunteered on a certain date. Do you keep a ledger with that information?"

"We do, and it's right on that table. You may sit there and look as long as you like. Please don't remove or mark on the pages."

Chuck turned the pages back until he found the date on which Zaida was murdered. He ran his fingers down the column until he spotted the name M. Branch. He knew she had to be Chris's wife. There would surely not be two people with the name Branch. To be sure, he turned two pages to the front. There was another M. Branch. He was certain she wasn't involved in any way. He was relieved.

"Thank you so much for your help," Chuck said with a smile as he touched his forehead. As he was exiting the building, he noticed a clock on the wall. It was already one o'clock and time for lunch. On the way to the school, he had noticed a small restaurant that specialized in Cuban sandwiches. When he arrived at the restaurant, he parked, went in and ordered the sandwich and a Coke. The food was excellent and the service good. He made a mental note to be sure to return.

It was two-thirty and Chuck knew he had at least an hour to put the information into the computer. He'd had the equipment for six months and didn't know what he'd do without it. As he typed, he thought he would give Mr. Spencer a call when he was finished. He took a Coke from the fridge and sat down to make the call.

The telephone rang several times. Finally, Mrs. Troxley answered. Chuck asked if he could speak to Mr. Spencer. He was told he left early to take his wife to the doctor. I hope she's all right. Chuck then asked if she would have Mr. Spencer call when it was convenient. She assured him she would give him the message.

It was after 5:00 p.m. when Spencer finally called Chuck. "Thanks for returning my call," Chuck said as he identified the caller. "How is Mrs. Spencer?"

"Chuck, she's near collapse. The doctor wanted to put her into the hospital, but she wouldn't hear of it. He gave her some tranquilizers. He advised her to seek grief counseling."

"I wanted to touch base with you to let you know things are moving along." Chuck had been on the case four days and he couldn't believe the progress ha had made.

Log: *Today I went to an elementary school to check out the volunteer list. Everything is fine. Called Preston Spencer. He had to take his wife to the doctor. Serious nerve problem. Doctor recommended grief counseling.*
CCW

11

The day of the Fraternal Order of Police deep sea fishing trip finally came and all who signed up to go anticipated a terrific day. The weather was excellent, not too hot or too cool. Due to the large number of participants, two boats would leave at the same time. Each would accommodate fifty to fifty-five fishermen.

Everything, even tackle was furnished. An open bar was provided. All kinds of food was available. The thing that really interested the men was the numerous prizes to be awarded. The categories were: largest fish caught, smallest, most unusual, first caught, regardless of size. An important prize had to be the cash given for a drawing when the boats docked in the afternoon. Everyone put their name on a slip of paper. The captain drew the name from a box. Moe and Jim decided to take different boats since they both expected to win the money.

Moe Garrett stood at the rail and talked to Aaron Clark, a traffic officer, whose tour of duty was usually completed on a Harley. The two men had much in common since they both rode, one for pleasure and one for his livelihood. They enjoyed a beer, but mostly they enjoyed the food and the refreshing salt air. Even though the two didn't win a prize, they enjoyed a wonderful day.

When the weekend over, Moe felt rested and ready to resume the Moore investigation. A cool morning encouraged him to park far back on the parking lot and enjoy a leisurely stroll to the building. As he approached the back door, he saw Aaron Clark heading to his motorcycle.

"Did you stop and get your fish from the grocery store, man?"

"Same as you. But didn't we have fun trying?"

"What you working today?" Moe asked.

"A funeral. I had to stop by to pick up some white gloves. John Patterson and I are working it together."

"Anyone we know?"

"No, it's a five year old named Joshua Davis. He's been fighting leukemia for over a year now, and he lost the battle last Thursday."

"Aaron, I know that family. I haven't heard from them lately, but when we were in high school George and Janice, Stacey and I doubledated some. We were in Viet Nam at the same time, but he was a long way from where I was stationed. A while back I was at the hospital investigating an agg assault. I knew Joshua was in the Pediatric Oncology Center, so I stopped in to say hello. You know I lost the end of my finger in a land mine explosion in Viet Nam."

"Yeah, I knew you were pretty banged up."

"Well, I have tried to use that loss to an advantage. I took my ball point pen and drew a smiley face on that finger. Then, I wiggled it down the sheet to him. He had the biggest smile you ever saw on a little face."

"You know Moe, I don't mind the funerals for old people. Sometimes, you even feel that death is a medicine that cures all pain. Now, when it's a little child, you can't help but feel such sadness for the family at the loss of the little one."

"You're so right. Did you know he had a teen aged sister? He was born long after George came home from the war."

"Well Moe, it's good to see you. I'd better be on my way. What do you think of our new bikes?"

"Man, they are the latest thing out. We didn't have 'em like that when I rode." Moe started to the door of the building and Aaron Clark cranked the cycle and threw up his hand as he pulled away to go direct traffic for the funeral procession. Moe remembered his traffic days when he rode all the time. He enjoyed every day, but Lou Ann was glad when that part of his career was over. She was much less worried with him in an unmarked sedan.

In the detective division, Moe listed the things that needed his attention. He left the department and headed east to interview a witness in an assault on a female. He turned on the radio and listened to the dispatches. Nothing significant came over and what did was a car theft that turned out to be a reposession almost before it was broadcast. Also, there was a runaway juvenile. All of a sudden, the message was loud and clear. "Officer down at Lake and 34th. All units in or near area report." Moe removed the radio, gave his location and told the dispatcher he was on his way. While remaining calm was part of his training, he dreaded what he knew was a strong possibility the downed officer was either Aaron or John. The location of the accident was on the route taken by the local funeral homes to the cemeteries in the area.

As a rule, using a motorcycle to direct traffic for a funeral procession is a rather cut and dried operation. The lead is stationed at the first intersection. He stays on his motorcycle at the center of the intersection with his lights flashing. The traffic stops. The cortege passes slowly with their lights on to show they are part of the procession. As the last car passes the officer, he falls in behind it, knowing the second officer has stopped traffic ahead. He then heads to the next intersection. You might say the officers are playing leap-frog at the intersections.

At Lake and 34th the procession was heading east. The officer pulled into the intersection and stopped at an angle. He was on the Harley with traffic stopped on his left. The driver of a heavy dump truck approaching on his right was headed straight for him. Without applying the brakes, the truck struck the officer who had no time for evasive action.

When Moe approached the intersection, he noticed the procession had temporarily halted. A traffic man had started to get the procession moving around what appeared to be a motorcycle lying on its side. He knew the rider must be seriously injured as no movement could be seen. A quick thinking Moe opened his trunk and removed a folded blanket he carried for just such emergencies. He ran to the downed officer. He could see there was little hope for the rider. The Harley was a heap of twisted metal and rubber. It appeared to have been hit solidly on the right side.

Aaron Clark was crumpled on his left side. Moe very carefully lifted his head and placed the blanket under it. He knew the officer and friend was critical, but thought he heard a sound coming from his mouth. He placed his ear near Aaron's mouth to try to hear what he was saying.

"Moe, I didn't know I'd see you so soon. I'm bad man. Tell Trish to take care of the boys, and I love her."

"It's done. Hang on. EMS is here now. You'll be fine." At that very minute, a limp head lying on the blanket on Moe's knee turned to the side. He knew his friend was gone, but said nothing as he was quickly put into the emergency vehicle. The traffic report read DOA or K as it was also called.

Chief Fallon decided to give the message to Trish Clark in person rather than take her to the hospital among strangers to be told the tragic news. When the chief and Moe arrived at

Who Killed Zaida Moore?

Aaron and Trish's home, she was not aware that an officer had been injured, even though the news had been on TV several times.

When the two men rang the doorbell, Trish answered the ring with "Oh no, Is Aaron okay?"

"Trish," began the chief, "may we come in?"

She opened the door and invited the men to come in and have a seat. Two little boys were hanging behind their mother. They had worried looks as if they expected bad news too.

"Maybe you'll want the boys to go into the den with their grandparents. Trish, the reason we're here is to tell you that Aaron was killed while he directed traffic for a funeral. I know this is so hard. It's painful for us too, but be aware we'll do everything we can to help you."

With that, Trish screamed and both men tried to comfort her with little success. The department had called Trish's parents and made sure they would be at their daughter's home when the chief came to give her the news.

The chief was visibly shaken when he tried to speak. "Trish, Detective Moe Garrett was with Aaron when the end came. He was able to speak enough to give Moe a message for you. I know it's hard, but I think you should hear it."

Moe, who was obviously distraught could hardly speak, but he knew the promise made to a dying comrade had to be kept. "Trish, I held Aaron's head and comforted him at the end. His dying words were, "Tell Trish to take care of the boys and I love her."

Trish held her mouth and screamed. Her mother and father could do little to help. The Chief and Moe stayed with her until a local physician, who had been called, arrived to give her something to help with her grief. Aaron's brother and sister-in-law came and Moe and the Chief felt they could then leave.

On the way back to the station, the two were silent. The chief finally spoke. "You know Moe, somewhere a policeman faces death daily. It goes with the profession, but this event should not have happened. The man who struck Aaron was a seventy-two year old driving a dump truck. Now you know no seventy-two year old needs to be driving that kind of heavy equipment."

"You're right Chief, but he did have a valid driver's license. He'll probably be charged with death by motor vehicle and placed on probation. What's really sad is that Clark's family was changed today. Never again will those two little guys look forward to Daddy throwing them up and catching them or going to the playground while Mommy shops for groceries."

Both men took their handkerchiefs and wipped tears flowing down their faces. They waited for a few minutes before they entered the building where today one less, brave, loyal, officer was counted.

Aaron Clark's funeral was held four days later and attended by officers from the entire state and some neighboring states as well. Even though the occasion was the ultimate in sadness, one would have to feel great pride in the outpouring of such fine uniformed peace officers. They wore their varied uniforms with grace and dignity.

Aaron's widow maintained the aura of one in deep mourning without the public display of wailing or sobbing, a countenance her beloved husband would have truly admired. She chose not to have the boys present as she thought the event would be unsettling for ones so young.

Chief Fallon, resplendent in his dress uniform, was the first to speak. Each word was meaningful and commanded total attention from all present. Part of what he said was dynamic, too meaningful not to repeat. "Family, friends, and fellow peace officers, today we meet at an event we pray we'll never have to attend. However, we humbly and thankfully are here to pay our final respects and a supreme tribute to a fallen comrade. Aaron Keith Clark was a twenty-eight year old who recently celebrated five years as a Tampa Police Officer. I remember a twenty-three-year-old, clear-eyed young man who was immensely proud to wear the uniform his paternal grandfather had worn over forty years before him. The family of Officer Clark has a long history of public service. Enough praise can't be given this peace officer.

We all know injuries, and even death, are daily possibilities, but we are still devastated when they occur. Our society and all mankind depend on all of you, the dedicated, honest men and women for our safety, peace and protection. We graciously accept the supreme sacrifice this young man has made. We will never forget you beloved friend and fellow officer."

When the U. S. flag and a small replica of the officer's badge was presented to his widow, there wasn't a dry eye in the assemblage of over six hundred officers. The memorable day would never be forgotten as Officer Aaron Clark was immortalized that day.

12

Moe pulled his unmarked car from his driveway. He had enjoyed a leisurely breakfast with Lou Ann and their daughter Mary Beth. He knew his work was cut out for him as he turned south onto Florida Avenue. He could have gotten on the Interstate, but he chose Highway 41 instead, turning left on Seventh Avenue. The east side of Tampa, once a pretty, tree-shaded, lower-middle income section, was now filled with drugs, drug dealers and other ne'er do wells. The police fought crime diligently, but generally unsuccessfully. No one in his right mind would choose to be there after dark.

Garrett slowed down near an apartment complex. In front near the street, two older men were playing checkers on a wooden cable spool they used for a table. Two worn orange crates served as seats. You could tell that competition was the name of the game, as no conversation passed between them. A younger African-American man stood beside them watching them match their checker wits.

"Are you Freddie Barnes?" He asked the young man standing there.

"Maybe I am and maybe I'm not," was his belligerent response.

"I don't want any of your horse shit," Garrett growled. "Just a little conversation. Say, you don't remember me, do you?"

"Can't say that I do."

"Two words, Big Mary, I think she's your twin sister."

Freddie Barnes didn't open his mouth except to say, "Let's go to my place."

Detective Moe Garrett followed him to the apartment complex. They went into the entrance and took the stairs to the second floor and Apartment 8. Freddie unlocked the door and motioned Garrett to go in. A woman and small child were sitting on the couch watching television.

"Grace, take Carinda over to your Mama's house. We have to talk some man talk." Without one word, the woman got up, picked up the little one and left the apartment.

"What's Big Mary up to?" Garrett asked making small talk.

"She's still picking fruit. Look, man, I'm sorry I didn't recognize you downstairs. Its been a long time."

"It has," Moe acknowledged.

"I knew that if it hadn't been for you, Mary would have gone to prison."

"You're right, Freddie, the law frowns on stabbing a person."

"She only stuck him a little."

"Now you know that she stuck him wide, deep and continuous. That scar on his face will go to the grave with him."

"Well, he didn't need to take her money off the table when she went to relieve herself."

"In other words, you think you ought to try to kill a person over thirty-five cents?"

"It's the principle of the thing," Freddie argued.

"I really didn't think we could have gotten a conviction anyway. Two witnesses said he twisted her arm before she pulled her knife and cut him. Let's get on with our talk."

"What is your full name?"

"My name is Freddie Eli Barnes."

"When were you born?"

"December 16, 1968, I think."

"What do you mean, I think?"

"I was born at home on either the sixteenth or seventeenth. My mama didn't have a calendar and didn't know the date. I took the sixteenth, Mary the seventeenth."

"Is this your legal address?"

"Yes, I live here with my baby and my baby's mama."

"Freddie, are you two married?"

"No, not legal, we're common law."

"Did you work for Mrs. Zaida Moore last week?"

"Yes, I work at the Moores' every Monday, Wednesday and Friday."

"Exactly what do you do at the Moore's residence?"

"I keep the yard, but mostly I keep about a half acre of roses. I spray, fertilize, and trim them. I also cut them for Miz Moore to take to the hospital. Them roses take two full days to keep good."

"Are you paid well for your work?"

"Not a whole lot, with the ADC me and Grace can get by pretty good."

"Who pays you?"

"Usually Mr. Moore pays me in cash. You know they rich," was Freddie's reply.

"I suppose if you say so. You do know that Mrs. Moore was found dead last Friday a week ago."

"I heard about it from the people who stay in the guest house."

"Were you at the Moores' the day she was found dead?"

"Yes, I worked until about 12:15. Mrs. Moore didn't like the roses messed with when it got real hot."

"What time did you get to the Moores' that day?"

"Around 7:30 a.m."

"Did you speak to Mrs. Moore?"

"Yes, I spoke to her when she come to the rose garden."

"Was she telling you something about your job?"

"No, I was almost finished by then. She said I could come into the house for a sandwich and a drink."

"Did you go into the house?"

"Yes, I carried the roses in for her. She had a sandwich and Dr. Pepper ready on the counter."

"How long were you in the house?"

"I really don't want to say," Freddie answered as he looked away.

"We're not talking about smoking a joint or being drunk and rowdy on the street, man. We're talking about murder one, with the victim being one of Tampa's wealthiest families. Do we talk here or downtown?"

"Will you not tell anybody less you just have to?"

"Freddie, I'm not a big mouth. I keep most things close to my chest," Detective Garrett replied. "You can make book on that."

"I'm embarrassed to tell you, but Miz Moore done come on to me before. The first time, she made a remark about my privates."

"Come on Freddie, you imagined that."

"No, honest, what she said was, was all my muscles as big as those on my arm here?" Freddie pointed to his arm.

"Well, what did you say or do?"

"I didn't say or do nothing. I acted like I didn't hear her. I had just finished cutting the roses and I walked back to the garden and acted busy."

"All this grabs me, but I'm interested in what happened Friday before last."

Freddie paused and seemed to be trying to collect his thoughts. "Well, I ate the ham sandwich and drank the Dr. Pepper. Miz Moore was drinking a drink. I think it was some kind of cocktail. She looked at me and said something about a tiger. I told her I seen a TV show that said sick old tigers would kill and eat people. She laughed and said I was a dumb ass, and what she was talking about was the tiger myth. She said it meant that black men had bigger tools than white men. You know what I mean, don't you Detective Garrett?"

A shocked Moe Garrett answered. "Yes, I know what you mean. Let's go on."

"Then, she asked me if I'd ever had sex with a white woman. I told her no, that I kinda stayed with my own color."

She said, "You don't know what you're missing."

"I sit that glass down so fast and got out of that house."

"How long would you say you were in the house?"

Freddie answered without hesitation, "It couldn't have been more than twenty minutes. I put my tools away and left."

"Did you see anyone as you left the Moore house?"

"I wasn't looking for anybody. I just wanted to get gone."

"Freddie, are you telling me that you didn't even think about screwing Mrs. Moore? She was beautiful."

"Maybe I thought about it, maybe for five seconds."

"I don't believe that."

"Detective Garrett, remember I asked you if you would tell anybody about our conversation. Well, there's something you should know. Grace, my baby's mama, is the only woman I ever been able to sket with."

Moe Garrett knew that sket meant to reach a sexual climax.

"I been to the doctor. He said it was psychological or something like that. Me and Grace been together over six years and we don't mess around with nobody else."

Moe Garrett couldn't hide a smile when he said, "Man, you need some of that new medicine the Japanese are testing."

"We're making it okay," was Freddie's reply.

"When you left the kitchen, was Mrs. Moore all right?"

"Yeah, she was arranging the roses to take to the hospital. That's why the bad news upset me so."

"Freddie, did you hurt Mrs. Moore?"

"No, I really liked her. She was good to me and Grace. She gave Grace some good clothes, and when Carinda was born, she gave her a present. I overlooked the sinful things she had in her mind."

"Now Freddie, you will probably be asked to take a lie detector test. I'll be in touch with you. Say hello to Big Mary for me. Tell her not to take her blade or heat with her when she goes to Rick's Bar." Detective Moe Garrett left Freddie Eli Barnes standing outside the door to his apartment. As he opened the car door, he looked up and waved at Freddie, who was holding his hand out in a friendly gesture.

The drive from the east side to the police department was only about ten minutes. It gave Moe time to think about where he would go with the information he had gotten minutes before. He decided he would request that the office manager, Robert Gonzalez, type the supplement with the sexual overtones. Since the report had to be checked out from Mr. Gonzalez's desk file, he felt comfortable enough to dictate the interview to him rather than using the method that would make it open to all stenos and clerks. Robert was the best typist in the whole department. His expression never changed as he typed. Reading from his notes, Detective Garrett dictated all that Freddie Eli Barnes had said. When they were finished, Mr. Gonzalez copied the supplement, gave Moe three copies and filed the original with the report. It was then returned to the locked drawer. The two men never communicated with one another except for the original greeting.

On the way out, Detective Garrett stopped by communications to give a copy to Captain Donavan. He read the supplement to himself and hit the edge of the paper with his fingertips. "Here's your man, Moe, it's as clear as glass."

"Now Moe, here's what I think really happened. Zaida, being the nice generous lady that she was, invited the yardman in to have something to eat and drink. You know how hot it was that Friday. She thought he would appreciate having a cool place to eat.

Freddie, no doubt, grabbed Zaida on the upper arms. He probably made sexual advances that frightened her. She tried to get away by running out the front door. He caught her at the door and struck her. He knew if she got outside, someone would surely come to her aid. Now think Moe, who would be carrying a heavy object, square in shape?"

"I haven't a clue."

"What was Freddie doing the day Zaida was killed?"

"Cutting roses for her to take to the hospital."

"I'm surprised at you, Moe. Freddie was cutting the roses with clippers. The sticky, fibrous rose stems dull clippers real fast. So he would have to sharpen them often."

"Well, what's next?"

"What do you sharpen anything, well almost anything, with? A whetstone."

"Jim, you may have something to look at further."

"Moe, all that trash talk that Freddie dealt you was to throw you off track. I've known Zaida for over twelve years and she's always been a perfect lady."

13

Moe thought about what Captain Donavan had said. He reflected on the original report that Officer Scott Johnson had written. In the report, the officer noted that the victim had what appeared to be little bruises on both upper arms. Nothing was mentioned about them on the autopsy report. Was it possible that Dr. Sheppard didn't think they were important since the death was the result of blunt force trauma to the lower back of the head. Detective Garrett walked around to the Patrol Division. He checked the duty roster and found that Officer Scott Johnson was assigned to Sergeant T. Jones. He was somewhere on duty at the time. Detective Garrett found Sergeant T. Jones in the cafeteria talking to two other officers. He waited until they were finished talking.

"Speak to you, Sergeant?" Garrett asked.

"Long time, no see, what have you been up to?"

"Man, I've been busy. You know I was assigned the Zaida Moore case."

"That doesn't surprise me, what can I do for you?"

"Officer Scott Johnson wrote the original report. Do you think I could talk to him?"

"Give me five minutes. He's working District One. Real handy."

"Can you have him meet me in the back parking lot?"

"No problem. He'll be driving Car 23 in case you don't know him. He hasn't been on the force long."

Moe was watching for Car 23 and when he spotted it, he pulled in beside it. He got out and opened the passenger side of the patrol car.

"Are you Detective Garrett?" questioned Officer Scott Johnson.

"I am, and I'm glad to meet you, Scott."

"I'm glad to meet you. I've heard a lot about you."

"Good, I hope," Moe said trying to play down the compliment.

"No one better in homicide, is what the inspector said."

"Do you remember the Zaida Moore murder?"

"I'll never forget it. It's the first murder report I originated. Sergeant Jones said I did a good job when he approved it."

"In the report, you stated that the victim showed small bruises on the upper arms."

"I surely remember those bruises. Mrs. Moore's skin was somewhat discolored, but the bruises still looked like fingers made them. You know what I mean, don't you?"

"Yeah Scott, over the years, I've seen a few."

"Is there anything else, Detective Garrett?"

"No, but I hope I didn't disturb you when you had something important going on. Thanks for the infomation."

"I'm glad to be of help and glad to meet you. Hope I see you around the station."

"I'll look for you." Moe said as he got into his unmarked car and headed to the loving arms of his wife and three year old daughter.

Police work is not always depressing and emotionally disturbing. Surely, by nature, policemen must deliver tragic messages about lost loved ones. They must give aid, comfort and protection to citizens who might be at death's door, not to mention protection of personal property against those in our society whose plan it is to take it from its rightful owner.

The job, though not always grim and giggles, is extremely rewarding. The well-educated, well-trained officers are equipped to handle all situations. The main criteria for employment as sworn personnel, and or civilians (as they are called) is and was excellence in performance of duty. Rarely do those employees fail to perform with integrity and efficiency. If your job was performed well, no one ever came down on you.

Humor can be found in all occupations, and the police department is no exception. Some nights when their tour of duty was over, many uniformed officers would meet in the cafeteria. One could never experience greater camaraderie anywhere. You might could call the meeting "Remember when?" as most of the conversations started with those two words. Some of those reminiscences were too good to leave untold. One such is as follows:

It seems that an officer on the north side was dispatched almost daily to the home of an elderly married woman who was obviously senile and mentally ill. She imagined that someone was coming into her house and stealing weird things like dish towels and varied foods. She even showed the officer where the culprit left sand on the floor. Her poor husband, old but not senile, just shook his head. The thoughtful officer knew that all people couldn't be put into mental institutions, even though they weren't well. What he came up with solved the problem.

He brought a legal sized manila envelope with her name and address typed on it. His instructions, also written on the envelope looked very official. They were: Sweep up the sand

and put it in the envelope. When the envelop is filled, an officer will come out, pick up the envelope and have the sand analyzed. Then they would arrest her thief. This pleased the woman and especially the husband. It was a brilliant idea and it worked The police never again had to investigate a theft of food or dish towels.

Some officers were very intuitive when on the street and never took chances. They felt it was better safe than sorry. Surely, there were officers that were injured and even killed in the line of duty, but generally those incidents were unavoidable. The safety record was excellent.

One area in which many officers could not be complimented was spousal fidelity. For some reason the men in blue attracted women like magnets attract iron shavings. Often the ladies would come to the station at night. Young, handsome, mostly married officers were tempted constantly

D.E. Joyner

14

Several days had passed since Detective Moe Garrett had done any work on the Zaida Moore case. He felt that if you gave a case a little rest, tongues would become active. The first thing he did after a few days was make a trip out Bayshore to the Moore residence. He called ahead to let Mark Pierce know he was on the way out. Pierce was waiting at the door of the guest cottage when Garrett parked the unmarked car.

"How have you been, Mr. Pierce?"

"Fair, and you?"

"Getting the job done, I guess."

"Let's go into the house. What brings you out here?"

Detective Garrett with a bit of anger in his voice said, "You weren't entirely truthful with me when I came out here last week."

"In what way?"

"You didn't tell me that you had a criminal record and had served time in a California state prison.

"I couldn't tell you that in front of Susan Parker."

"Well, where is she now? You know she wasn't supposed to leave without notifying me of her intentions."

"She left for Nashville on Sunday. Her husband gave her an ultimatum, either she come home, or she would be moved out. Since Zaida had died, she felt that there was no future here. She said she never wants to see me again."

"That's strange behavior?"

"Not for her. She can't be true to one man for long. She likes a lot of variety."

"Another thing, what did you serve time for in California?"

"Don't bullshit me, detective, you know why I served time."

"Okay, so I know. I also know too, that several pieces of jewelry belonging to Zaida Moore are missing. Two rings on the insurance schedule have a combined value of over twenty thousand dollars. You know you couldn't move them here. We have a pawn detail that's been nationally recognized. Also, we have effective snitches on every corner."

"Are you accusing me of stealing jewelry from my host and hostess?"

"That's exactly what I'm accusing you of. Now lets talk business. There's no reason for me to keep you here since you are obviously not involved in Zaida Moore's death. But, I want those rings now, this minute."

"I don't have them and you can't prove that I do."

Detective Garrett spoke firmly, "No, I can't prove that you have them, but I can arrest you for investigation of grand theft. By the time you could prove your innocence, you'd be so broke you'd have to hitchhike out of town. I mean what I'm saying."

Not one word passed between the two men for a painfully long time. Ever the gentleman, Mark Pierce intoned, "Will you excuse me please?" He was gone for a short period. When he returned and faced Detective Garrett he said, "Here." Garrett held out his hand and Mark David Pierce thrust two of the most beautiful diamond rings he had ever seen into it.

Mark had a scowl on his handsome face as he asked, "What now?"

"I want you to get the hell out of Dodge now. If you're here after twenty-four hours, it's three-thirty now, you'll personally answer to me."

As Moe pulled out of the driveway, he felt he had accomplished one thing. He saw to it that a known jewel thief was going somewhere else to ply his trade. Garrett regretted that he couldn't arrest him, but after he returned the rings, there was no chance Moe could charge him with anything.

Garrett stopped by communications to show Captain Donavan what he had in his pocket. The two walked together to the property room and got a receipt for two diamonds set in platinum, approximate value $22,500. Captain Donavan said he would notify Bob Moore to come by and pick up his deceased wife's property.

15

It had been two weeks and Garrett knew he had to revisit Freddie, he dreaded it. Freddie had left him feeling good about his innocence; however, Captain Donavan had caused him to be wishy-washy about his first impression. With this in mind, Garrett turned on Seventh Avenue and headed east. He didn't call Freddie to make an appointment because he thought an unexpected visit would produce better results.

As Moe pulled in front of the apartment complex, it was like déjà vu. The same two men were playing checkers on the same cable spool table, sitting on the same worn orange crates. They didn't speak, but they were watching Garrett closely as he walked toward the apartment entrance.

"He ain't home," one of the checker players called out.
"You don't happen to know where he is, do you?"
"Is this Wednesday?" the checker player asked.
"Yes it is."
"He at the job today."
"You mean the garden keeper job on Bayshore?"
"Yeah, that his job, the one on Bayshore."

Garrett groaned at the thought of driving all the way through town and out Bayshore. He got into his car and started the trip.

Sure enough, he found Freddie in the rose garden. He was soaking the ground around the bushes. He looked up when he saw the car pull into the driveway.

"What you doing here?" he asked as he walked toward the car.

"There's a few things we need to talk about. It won't take long."

"We can sit under the trees," Freddie said as he led the way to a beautiful sitting area. The raised fifteen-foot square patio was the same red brick as those used for the drive. A two-foot wall was raised to five feet at each corner. Beautiful black lantern-like lamps were on each corner. The table and chairs were stone and gray marble.

The two men settled down and Detective Garrett started to talk. "I'm surprised to see you back here working so soon after Mrs. Moore died."

"These roses have to be cared for, period. Mr. Moore said I could take the ones cut home with me. Man, people love to see me coming with them flowers."

"Remember when we met two weeks ago, Freddie?"

"Sure, I do. I remember what we talked about too."

"Would you go over again what you did on the day Mrs. Moore was murdered."

"Well, I cut probably five or six dozen roses."

"What type of clippers do you use to cut them?"

"I use a stainless steel clipper."

"Does it stay sharp to cut all the roses?"

"Oh no, I have to sharpen it several times during my cuts."

"What do you use to sharpen the clippers?"

"Detective Garrett, I use a whetstone like you'd use to sharpen a pocket knife." He answered the question with a sense of pride at his superior knowledge on the subject. "It knocks the sticky fiber off the blades of the clippers."

"Do you use the same one each time?"

"Yep, been using it for a long time."

"Do you mind if I see your whetstone?"

"I'll get it. It's in with the garden supplies in the storage shed. When I cut the roses, I carry it in my pocket." Freddie hurried back with the whetstone. When Moe saw it, he nearly swallowed his tongue. The whetstone was almost three inches wide, five inches long, and just over an inch thick. He thought about the autopsy and what Captain Donavan had said about the murder weapon. He asked if he might take the whetstone with him to the police department.

"Sure," Freddie said, "I have a file that I can use until you bring me back my whetstone."

"I'll try to get it back to you in a day or two."

Freddie walked with him to the car, talking as they walked. Moe Garrett couldn't collect his thoughts so he said, "I'll see you, man."

He placed the whetstone in his handkerchief and put it on the seat beside him glancing at it occasionally. It almost seemed to be something sinister.

When he got back to the station, he immediately went to see Captain Donavan. He took the whetstone from his handkerchief and placed it on the desk in front of the Captain.

"Well, I'll be damned, its just what I thought. Moe, take that straight to the lab for testing. Fortunately, we now have updated equipment that can assist in solving many crimes."

"I know and I hope this is one of them."

Captain Donavan, feeling a little smug, opened his drawer, took out a cigar, ripped off the cellophane, bit the end off it, and struck his Zippo lighter at the other end. He grabbed Moe's arm and said, "Boy, I'm going to have to teach you a thing or two about solving murders."

"Go to hell, Jim, we don't have anybody in booking yet."

"No, but we will have soon. Take my word for it."

Moe made his getaway before the captain's cigar had a chance to fill his office with foul smelling smoke.

Entering the records section, Moe was met by Robert Gonzalez. "Good morning Detective Garrett, anything for the Moore file?"

"No, but maybe in a day or two. You still have that locked in your desk, don't you?"

"Oh yes. As a matter of fact even the mayor doesn't have access to my desk file. The lock was made special. It's not one of those little keys that come with office furniture. The chief has a key and I have one."

"You're a good man, Robert," Garrett said to the fellow Hillsborough High School graduate. The two men went back a long way. Actually Robert Gonzalez had been with the department for years. He was sworn personnel, which meant he was a police officer, but he didn't flaunt it, as his clerks and stenos made a fraction of his salary.

At the rotary file, Sally was filing complaint cards from the night before.

"Mind looking something up for me?"

"For you, Moe, anything."

"Anything?" Moe questioned.

"You know what I mean. Have you heard any good jokes lately?"

"Nah, I've been too busy with the Moore murder."

"I'm at your service. What can I do for you?"

"Look up Freddie Eli Barnes B/M D.O.B 16 December 65."

Sally pushed the "B" button and the rotary spun around and stopped. "Barnes, Barnes, Freddie Eli. We don't have a lot of Barnes," she mused as she flipped through the cards. "Oh yes, here he is. Want his Tampa Police Department Number?"

"Let me have it. Anything on his defendant card?"

"Not much, but he has been arrested."

"That figures, what for?"

"Vandalism (car window), carrying a concealed weapon, grand larceny-looting (case dismissed). Nothing major, nothing at all for the past five years."

"He's got a lady now and you know a good woman can make a man good."

"Moe, I seem to get all the bad men. I'm on number three, and he's out the door soon."

"Don't do anything rash," Detective Garrett advised. "I'm going to I.D. and check Barnes out."

16

As Moe made his way to the detective division from the Identification Section, he thought about the rap sheet of Freddie Barnes. There was nothing to indicate he was anything but a petty law breaker. He had absolutely no sex related crimes reported. He wasn't a thief, that is one who had been arrested. Also, he had been squeaky clean for over five years. Moe knew people can and do change. Many of his cases had been solved by arrests of suspects never before fingerprinted. It's possible Freddie would be counted among the lesser known, those who commit a crime of passion. All these possibilities were tumbling around in his gray matter, but he still couldn't see Freddie as a killer

Moe entered the door as Chief Fallon walked out headed to his office down the hall. The men spoke and each went on to his destination. Inspector Bridges met Moe as he entered and requested him to come into his office. He had some information he thought would add something to the Moore murder investigation.

The chief had a call earlier from the owner-manager of the Sanitary Pest Service. He said he had read the article in the paper of the death of Mrs. Moore. He was certain she was a customer of the pest control service. His company, although not large, was expanding, and now served over six hundred homes each month. He had his assistant pull the records for the day of the murder and surely enough, they were signed by Z. Moore. Several months earlier he had the time of arrival and completion of service added to the tickets. This enabled him to justify the need for more service personnel and to be sure he was getting his moneys worth from all employees.

Inspector Bridges thought Moe might benefit from a visit to the company to interview the operator that served the Moore home on the day of the murder. Moe wasn't too optimistic, but he knew a suggestion from the chief demanded immediate attention. He didn't mind the drive out John F. Kennedy Boulevard. The Sanitary Pest Service was located about five miles from the police department. The business operated from a warehouse with the front remodeled for an office. The back of the building held supplies needed to perform various pest exterminations. Moe pulled into the parking area next to the company sign.

He entered the front door and noticed two ladies seated behind computers. He hardly had time to speak before a man was in front of him.

"I'm Lee Nolan. I spoke to the chief earlier today and he assured me you would be interested in our record of the Moore service on the day she was murdered. You are Detective Moe Garrett, aren't you?"

"I am." Moe responded wondering if he looked the part so much, he needed no introduction.

"Come into my office. I have the service associate available."

The two men shook hands and Moe followed Mr. Nolan into his office. A lady dressed in the uniform of the pest service was seated. She looked efficient, but not too friendly.

"Detective Garrett, I want you to meet Debra Bryan. She was one of the first people I hired when I started the business. I trust her in all matters concerning recording the tickets. Her integrity is unquestioned.

"I'm glad to meet you, Detective Garrett. I hope I can be of some help to you."

"It's a pleasure. I thank you for being willing to be interviewed. Now, exactly what time did you arrive at the Moore house?"

"We keep tickets on every service call. I have mine available. You may see it."

She handed Moe the ticket she had filled out completely on the day of the service.

"Is 11:50 the correct time, Ms. Bryan?"

"Absolutely."

"Do you mind telling me what you did and where you were in the house on the day listed on this ticket."

"When I first got to the house, I rang the doorbell at the back door. Mrs. Moore came to the door, unlocked it, and invited me in. I asked her if she had a problem and she said, 'Not really, but you can spray a little around the work area where I do my roses. Sometimes I bring insects in from the garden.' I asked her if the outside needed any attention? She said, 'It always needs attention.' I sprayed around the sink and left by the back door after Mrs. Moore unlocked it. I was probably in the house no more than five minutes."

Moe was taking notes and paused to finish what he was writing. "Did you see anyone near, or around the house?"

"Yes, as I started to spray the foundation, a car pulled out and left down the driveway."

"Did you notice the driver of the car?"

"There were two people. A man was driving with a woman passenger."

Who Killed Zaida Moore?

"You know the Moores had a gardener. He worked on the day Mrs. Moore died. Did you see him?"

"Yes, I saw him. He was in the rose garden. I think he was cutting roses. He had a basket with a bucket of water in it on the ground and was putting the cut roses into it. About the time I finished my service, Mrs. Moore was walking to the house from the rose garden. The yardman was carrying the basket."

"What did you do then?" Moe inquired.

"I put my sprayer into the back of the van, got into it and drove away from the house."

"What time does the ticket show you completed the service?"

Debra handed Moe the ticket. He read aloud, "12:05 p.m. Are you sure of this time?"

"My Seiko keeps perfect time. I looked down at it as I was writing the ticket. I entered what I had sprayed and if I thought there was a problem that might require a return service."

"Did you notice where the gardener had parked his car?"

"I'm not sure, but there was a green Honda parked on the far drive in front of the utility shed."

"Ms. Bryan, I thank you for your time. Mr. Nolan, it's nice to meet you. The chief sends his thanks for you help. Will you copy this ticket for me, please?"

When Moe got into his car, he took time to review his notes. He felt the time sequence of the crime fit in with the time Freddie was admittedly in the house. Debra Bryan removed any doubt about Mark Pierce and Susan Parker. They both had the perfect alibi, but weren't aware of it.

On his way back to the station, Moe was really confused about the interview with Debra Bryan. She put Freddie at the scene. The chief was right on target when he said he thought the visit to Sanitary Pest Service could fill in some missing links.

17

Chuck knew the most important interview was still waiting to be held. He had been on the case for almost a week and had put a few things together about the murder and its possibilities. He really dreaded facing a man who had lost his wife and was still grieving for the loss. He steeled himself and called the number listed on the offense report. Chuck was about to hang up, when a man answered. The voice sounded hollow and weak. Chuck identified himself and asked to speak to Mr. Robert Moore. Chuck was told the voice was that of Bob Moore. He then advised Bob Moore he had been retained by Mr. Preston Spencer to add to the police investigation. If possible, he would like to speak to him to clarify a few questions. To his surprise, Bob agreed to see him immediately. Within ten minutes, Chuck was headed out Bayshore to the Moore residence.

He parked on the driveway and walked to the front door. He hit the doorknocker and the door was opened promptly.

"Are you Mr. Moore?" Chuck asked as he removed his badge case for the man to observe his credentials.

"I am," Bob responded as he opened the door for Chuck to enter.

"Thanks for seeing me. I'm Chuck Wilson."

Who Killed Zaida Moore?

"I spoke with Preston a few days ago and he told me he had hired additional help to find out who killed Zaida. I told him at the time the police were doing all they could and to be patient. He could not be dissuaded, so I told him I'd pay half of your fee. He advised me he could handle it alone. Have a seat Mr. Wilson. Can I get you something to drink?"

"No, thank you. I will be taking notes, but don't let it bother you. They're for my benefit when I enter the information into the computer."

"I've been expecting you. I was told you would probably be coming by. My best friend is a captain at the Tampa Police Department. He, too, is disappointed an arrest hasn't been made in the murder."

"Before we start the interview, do you mind if I walk out the back door and enter the house exactly as you did the day your wife died?"

"Sure, follow me," Bob accommodated.

"Now tell me exactly what time you came home and what happened."

Bob thought for a while and answered slowly. "I came home about two-fifteen. I didn't see anyone at the apartment as I opened my car door. As you can see, you are facing the building and automatically look in that direction. I came through the back door and service porch.

"Let me stop you for a minute. Did you have to use a key, or was the door open?

"I used my key that I removed from my pocket."

"When you entered the house was anything out of place?"

"No, nothing was out of place."

"You're at the kitchen door, coming through the service porch. Is that right?"

"That is correct."

"You are coming into the back of the room which has a utility kitchen separated by a lowered ceiling, correct?"

"Right. I looked to the left and Zaida's roses were being arranged at the sink. Since she wasn't there, I assumed she was in the powder room or using the phone in her office. I called, but didn't get an answer. I didn't think anything about it. I opened the fridge and took out a Coke. I started into the family room through the hall. When I got into the room, I could see Zaida's pants beside the staircase."

"Mr. Moore, what did you do then?"

"I ran and knelt down beside her. I called her name and rubbed her face. I could see that she wasn't breathing and her face was pale." Bob was distraught and the interview had to be halted temporarily.

"Then, did you call 911?"

"Yes, and I called my good friend Jim Donavan."

"When the EMTs arrived, did you have to unlock the front door?"

"I did."

"What type lock do you have on that door?"

"It's a deadbolt."

"Where was the key to the door?"

"We keep the key in that urn there beside the door."

"Were all keys accounted for at the time?"

"As far as I know."

"Mr. Moore, what type of clothing was your wife wearing on the day she was killed?"

"She was wearing black wide-legged slacks and a tan top."

"When you found you wife. Were her clothes disheveled?"

"No, she looked like she had laid down for a nap. She even had on her shoes."

Chuck could visualize a body on the couch being pulled under the arms to the staircase and let go. The clothing would have been down, probably more than from just walking. All wrinkles would have been pressed out. If she had fallen down the stairs, the slacks and loose top could have been forced up around the bust and knees.

"Mr. Moore, do you think any of your firends could have committed this crime?"

A thoughtful Bob answered, "All our friends are of long standing. I can't think of one capable of such an act."

"How can you be sure of that? You never know what's in a person's mind?"

"Let's just say I don't think we know anyone who would commit murder."

"Okay, now that's better. Now, did you two get along well?"

"Yes, we rarely disagreed. We were both caring and sharing."

"Mr. Moore, this house is opulent. Can I assume you two were wealthy?"

"I've been fortunate to be quite successful. We have always had more than enough."

"Is Zaida's family also well to do?"

"Mr. Wilson, Zaida came from a wonderful, loving family. Her father is a smart attorney who didn't aspire to great wealth. I would say they are comfortable."

"Have you ever had an extramarital relationship?"

"No, I never needed one."

"Is there anything you can add to the interview that might help with the investigation?"

"No, but if you'll leave your card, I'll call you if I think of anything."

Chuck stood and Bob Moore walked him to the door. He couldn't get the image of someone being dragged about eight feet from the couch, and being let go at the bottom of the stairs out of his mind. He didn't consider Bob, but he did think the perp was a man as it would have been difficult for most women to move a rigid body that far.

Chuck knew detectives don't necessarily appreciate private investigators, but he wanted to discuss a few things with Moe Garrett. He decided to call the police department and invite Moe to lunch. Moe had no plans, so they decided to meet at a downtown cafeteria. After they had eaten, they started to discuss the Moore case.

"Chuck, you were a police officer too, weren't you?"

"Yes Moe, I loved law enforcement, planned to make it my life's work. Fate intervened and here I am."

"Can you talk about it, or is it too sensitive?"

"It's been five years now, so I'm no longer bitter. Here's exactly what happened. No holds barred. It's not a pretty story. I'll warn you before I start."

"I can handle it," Moe assured him.

"I usually worked midnights a long way from where my wife and I lived. Due to several absences, I was given an assignment close to my neighborhood. Since I was so close to my house, I decided to stop by and say hello to my wife and get something to drink. I noticed a strange car in our driveway and thought she had one of her girlfriends over. I let myself in and wished a thousand times I had never turned that key. My wife and a fellow officer were cuddled up on the couch. When she saw me, she jumped up and ran to the bathroom. He was in a state of shock just looking at me. I reached over and picked up his hand. I put it close to my nose and all doubt was removed. I drew my weapon and gave him five seconds to move or I'd kill him. Moe, I would surely have done it, but something kept me from cocking that revolver. My wife came out of the bathroom and the urge was too strong. I slapped her so hard across her face. Her eye swelled shut almost instantly, and her face was swollen and bruised.

When I had finished my tour of duty at 0645 hours and returned to the station, she was in the sergeant's office. My captain was called in and pictures were taken of her face. Personnel demanded my resignation on the spot. I didn't have a leg to stand on as the department has zero tolerance for spousal abuse. My family, my home, my life were gone in one fell swoop. Moe, as a homicide detective, you are aware of cases like mine. I really am sorry I struck her, but I couldn't contain myself. It was truly a lapse of judgement on my part."

"Chuck, you know I'm human and I too have my unknown limitations."

"Thanks, Moe."

"Well Chuck, let's talk about the Moore case. What's happening?"

"Moe, I've been staying pretty busy. The one thing that bothers me is the position of the victim at the time of death."

"In what way?"

"See what you think? She was facing the wall. Her face was almost completely touching the carpeted floor. Do you think she died elsewhere and was dragged to the foot of the stairs?"

"Yes, that is surely a possibility. I'm going to carefully study the crime scene photos."

"Another thing, Bob Moore said the door was locked with a deadbolt and he unlocked it to let the EMT's in. Don't you think this would mean the killer came in through the back door? Moe, you know I wouldn't violate a trust, but maybe you should talk to Mrs. Estelle Knight. Her property joins the Moore's at the back."

Moe thought back to what the chief had said about Chuck not knowing a whorl from a tented arch. He totally underestimated this private investigator.

Log:*Interviewed Bob Moore. He was nice and cooperated with me. I got the impression that he was holding something back from me.*

Moe Garrett and I had lunch together. We shared some facts that are evident in the Moore murder. He's a good guy.

I do have an idea of an experiment I'm going to try.
CWW

18

Chuck couldn't shake from his mind the position Bob Moore said Zaida was lying in when he found her. He knew the crime scene crew had made photos of every angle. He also knew that a body will shift and sometimes move about during the death process. This would have caused the clothing to be in disarray. Sometimes arms and legs flail about and muscles reflex automatically as life leaves the body. Any of these actions would have caused clothing not to be smoothed down when in the prone position. If Chuck could only see the crime scene photos, he could evaluate the total picture. He knew that was not possible as an arrest hadn't been made and any tampering with evidence could hamper due process.

A thought came into Chuck's head like a beam of light. If he could find a woman of average weight and height to go along with his idea. The plan was to re-enact falling down the stairs and being pulled from one place to another. He considered where he would find such a woman and what she should be wearing.

As he was going to his condo, he passed the Goodwill store where he had bought some things for his apartment. He turned around and parked. He thought he had seen some clothes that might work when he was there before. He entered the store and was immediately approached by a clerk.

"May I help you Sir," she said?

"Yes, I'm looking for a pair of slacks with wide legs. I think they need to be rather stylish."

"What size are you looking for?"

"I'm not sure, but the lady is about your size. If you don't mind, would you show me some."

"Now sometimes I wear a ten, but to be on the safe side, maybe you'd better get a twelve," she admitted.

The clerk pushed the slacks down the rack one pair at a time. She finally removed a pair of black slacks from the rack. "Do these look like what you need?" she asked.

"I don't want them to be too slick or too rough like denim," he answered.

"These are like new, they're a blend, completely washable. They will hold a crease. Do you think they'll do?"

"They look fine to me. Do you have a loose fitting top that would go with black?"

The clerk was very helpful and appreciated such a nice customer. She led him to a rack with blouses and tops, stopped and started to separate the tightly packed garments. "I love black and tan together. You can dress it up or down. Think she'd like the combination?"

"Probably, what size do you think I should get?"

"I wear a twelve. If they come in small, medium or large, I'd buy a medium."

"Let's look at that size. Thank you so much for your help."

"No problem," she said as she pulled a beige and black top from the rack. How does this one look?"

"Is it loose at the bottom?"

"Look for yourself. It more than goes around me and it's a medium."

"You know, I kinda like the combination. I'll take them."

The helpful clerk agreed. "They do look good."

Chuck paid a total of ten dollars plus tax for the outfit. He asked the cashier if they needed cleaning and was told that everything was cleaned before it was sold.

Usually you buy clothes to fit the woman, but Chuck had to find a woman to fit the clothes. Finding the right size would present no problem. Finding one who would buy into the plan was something else.

When Chuck arrived at his apartment, he looked around and thought the space available was perfect. He knew he'd have to pull the couch out about five feet. No problem. He knew when he approached a woman, he'd have to be very careful. The idea had 'kook' written all over it. He finally decided he'd sit in his car outside his apartment. Plenty of women who'd fill the bill would pass by.

It was five o'clock and Chuck knew many condo residents would be coming home soon. He was reading a book and looking up over the top of it at the walkway where a lady might pass. One who looked like she would fill the bill passed by. He bailed from the car and was beside her instantly. "Excuse me, Miss. Would you like to earn fifty dollars for a little acting job?"

The about twenty-five year old said in a loud voice, "What kind of a pervert are you?" She hurried to her condo without looking back.

Chuck thought, number one down the drain. He took his former position and waited for number two. She walked by quickly and when approached, didn't look right or left. Needless to say, he was a little discouraged, but not ready to give up yet.

Finally, a cute bouncy gal came along. Chuck decided to use a different approach. "Miss, I'm looking for a model to pose for a magazine. Do you think you would be interested?"

"What magazine?" The young girl asked excitedly.

"It's a trade magazine. If you're right for the job, there could be much more," a lying, fast thinking Chuck said.

"Is the pay good?"

"If you work out, it's fifty dollars an hour."

"Wow, that's a lot. Can I bring my boyfriend?"

"You can bring the pope if you like, but he must stay out of the way while we work."

"Let me change clothes and I'll be right back."

Chuck reached for his camera case and got out of the car. He waited in front of it for his new hire to return. When she came back, she had a young man in tow. He was neat and looked like a young salesman.

They went into Chuck's condo and introduced themselves. The future model was Nancy and her boyfriend was Mike. Chuck never used his name under these circumstances, but used a pseudonym. The one he used was 'Nosliw' which is Wilson spelled backward. He pronounced it Noslew. This was handy and easily remembered.

He handed Nancy the bag with the clothes in it and showed her to the bathroom where she might change into the model attire. When she came back, she complained the pants were too large. Chuck had anticipated such a problem and purchased a card of safety pins. He took the pins from the bag, handed them to her, and told her to take the pants up, pin them to fit and pull the top down over them. When she pulled the top down, her ensemble looked great. She was ready for the shoot.

Her boyfriend, Mike, was sitting on a chair watching the very professional performance. The first pose was of Nancy lying on the couch with her head almost buried in the upholstery.

Who Killed Zaida Moore?

Chuck yelled camera and she froze. He took several angles of the position. When satisfied with the exposures, he had her go to the top of the stairs.

"Come on Mike, I need your help for this take."

Mike had really gotten into it and welcomed the chance to help. He waited for Chuck to explain what they would shoot. "Here's what we'll do. We'll get her by the arms and pull her down the stairs. We'll be very careful so there's no chance of her being injured. You're strong."

Nancy lay down on the landing with her arms down beside her head. The two men slowly pulled her down the stairs. They held her wrists firmly. When they had her completely down the stairs, they let her go. Chuck yelled "Camera" and she hardly breathed. He took several shots of the pose and was pleased with the results

Shot number three was a little more difficult. Nancy had to lie down on the couch. Her position was basically the same as number one, but she held her arms out slightly. Chuck came in front of her and put his arms under hers. He pulled her from the couch and dragged her to the area at the foot of the stairs. He eased her down, grabbed the camera and yelled, "still." He took several shots from different angles. He was pleased with the entire scenario and knew the developed photos would reinforce his thinking about the death scene.

He thanked his model and handed her a fifty dollar bill. "Mike, I couldn't have done it without you. Here's twenty dollars for your help."

Nancy was excited with her new profession. "If you need me again, Mr. Noslew, you can call me. I'm leaving you my phone number."

"Thank you so much for the twenty. I'm a part time salesman in the camera department at the drugstore. I go to school full time. This will come in handy," Mike said.

He knew the two appreciated the money, but they had no idea what it meant to him. He was eager to get the film developed, but to be on the safe side, he decided to take it to a drug store a little out of town. He got into his car and headed out Dale Mabry. After about ten miles, he spotted a drug store and pulled into the parking lot. When he filled out the envelope, he wrote John Nosliw on the customer line.

Chuck felt his day had been productive as he drove through KFC, picked up dinner and headed home. He rearranged his furniture and settled down to watch a ball game on television.

Log:
I hope I'm not jumping to conclusions. I re-enacted the scene Moe Garrett and I talked about. I left the film at a drugstore a safe distance from my residence.
CWW

Who Killed Zaida Moore?

19

Chuck was driving around the Moore neighborhood and came to the end of Bayshore Boulevard. On the left, he noticed the bay came close to the street. He stopped and got out to look it over. He could see a pier and a small restaurant. He went up to the counter and ordered a sandwich and a drink. He sat at a picnic table from where he could see the pier and the people fishing. He thought it was the most resfull environment he had been in. He parked and got out to look it over. He spotted a little restaurant and decided to have lunch there. Lunch was good and the park had a pier from which several people were fishing. He thought the park was the most restful environment he'd been in in a long time.

Around five-thirty, Chuck looked at his watch and decided to head out Dale Mabry to pick up the film he'd left the day before. He discovered the first negative thing about Tampa. The traffic was heavy and slow moving. You had to be a heads up, aggressive driver to get anywhere. He was in no big hurry and took his time reaching the drugstore.

He entered the store and stopped at the front counter. "Pictures for John Nosliw?"

The clerk pulled the picture drawer out and checked the envelopes. "Here it is, sir. That will be eleven fifty."

Chuck handed him a twenty and was given his change. "Thank you Mr. Nosliw. I hope you like them."

"I'm sure I will. Thank you." he answered. He wanted to look at the pictures immediately, but decided to wait until he got home where had a magnifying glass. He had sandwich meat and cheese in the refrigerator, so he headed straight home.

His dining table, with a bright light over it, was the perfect place to really examine his evidence. He placed his sandwich and glass of milk on the far side of the table out of the way. He opened the envelope and removed the pictures. He couldn't believe his eyes. They were perfect, each and every one. Even his model had a realistic look.

The first shot of her on the couch looked as if she were pushed down hard with her head jammed into the upholstery material. In one shot, her eyes were closed and she actually looked dead or unconscious.

Pose number two was the most realistic shot of them all. The clothing she wore told the story. Her top was up under her arms. It was so far up, it actually exposed her bra. The waist of her pants was not moved, but the large pants legs were above her knees. You could definitely tell she had been upside-down. Chuck was so excited he could hardly contain himself.

Pose number three told the tale. The pictures looked as if Nancy, the model, had laid down and smoothed her clothes out. There wasn't one wrinkle in the whole outfit. All three poses showed exactly what Chuck wanted them to show, but pose number three was absolute proof that Zaida was killed somewhere else and dragged to the foot of the stairs. The murderer never thought of how moving the body would change her clothing.

Chuck studied the exposures with his magnifying glass. He was certain these pictures would change the thinking about the murder and murderer. He wanted to share his findings with

Who Killed Zaida Moore?

Moe Garrett, but was apprehensive about how they would be received. He finally decided to call Moe the next morning.

Chuck finished his dinner and settled down to read the newspaper. He couldn't get his mind off the pictures. He took them out and examined them again.

Log: *Today I picked up the posed pictures from the photo shop. They are excellent and tend to show positively the victim did not fall down the stairs. Also, the victim was probably not killed at the place and position described by the husband when the offense was written.*
CWW

Early the next morning, Chuck called the detective division at Tampa Police Department and left word to have Detective Garrett call him. His call was returned about ten o'clock. He was on his way to the police department when the call came. The two decided to met in the cafeteria at ten-thirty. They met and sat at the rear of the restaurant.

"Detective Garrett, I think you'll be interested in what I brought with me," Chuck announced.

"Well what is it?" questioned Moe.

"Do you remember when we talked about the position of the victim?"

"I do. We talked about the crime scene investigators and the shots they had taken, right?"

"Right. Let me tell you what I did two days ago. I hired a young lady to pose exactly as Bob Moore said his wife was when he found her. I bought pants and a top like he said she was wearing. I posed her and took pictures. Then her boyfriend and I pulled her down the stairs and let her down easy at the landing.

I took multiple shots of that scene. You know Bob Moore still thinks she fell down the stairs," Chuck added.

"I know, I've really had a hard time trying to convince him the coroner said it couldn't have happened that way."

"Okay, Moe. The first two poses were very effective, but the third was, without question, the most perfect you ever saw."

"Do you have the shots with you?" Moe inquired.

"That's the reason I'm here," Chuck said as he lifted his briefcase and placed it on his lap. He opened it and removed the envelope containing the photos. "Let me explain as you view each shot. I'll spread them out on the table."

Moe examined each photo. He closely looked at the one with the face pushed into the couch. "How does this figure into the murder scene?" he inquired.

"In theory, the murder could have been committed on or near the couch in the living room."

"I don't see your point." Moe answered.

"I think you will when you've seen the rest of the shots," Chuck answered.

"For shot number two, the model's boyfriend and I had her lie down on the upstairs landing. He and I took her wrists firmly and pulled her down the stairs. At the bottom, we eased her into a prone position. Notice the way her clothes are fitting," Chuck said pointing his pen to the slacks and top.

Moe asked, "Did you turn her loose and let her collapse naturally at the bottom of the stairs?"

"We did. The only fallacy could be that she was a little conscious of her safety when we eased her down. If you notice, the pants are up above the knees, and the top actually exposes the bottom of her bra. If the victim had fallen down the stairs, the clothing would have been similar to this photo. See what I mean?"

Who Killed Zaida Moore?

"Chuck, there is one mitigating factor to be considered. The angle of the steps would affect the way the clothing became disarrayed."

"I thought about that. My stairs are probably a little steeper than those I observed at the Moore home, but not enough to make a tremendous difference."

"I see exactly what you mean, Chuck."

"Wait until you see number three. You are going to be surprised."

"Let's have a look at it."

"Before you look at it, I want to explain it to you. Bob Moore said Zaida's clothing was smoothed down when he found her. If, in fact, she had died at the bottom of the stairs, she would have shown some reflex. Look at these shots. Her clothing is flawless. Not a wrinkle anywhere. See what I mean?" Chuck explained.

"You're right. We could superimpose a picture of Zaida's head and it would be almost the exact copy of the crime scene photos," a surprised Moe answered.

"Here's how I affected the shot. I had my model lie down on the couch. Her arms were slightly out. I put my hands under her arms from the front and pulled her off the couch to the stair position. Then, I let her down easy. She did not move or touch her clothes. I ruled out a woman murderer since most women wouldn't have the strength to move a rigid body which is dead weight."

"Here's what I think happened. I feel that Zaida was killed elsewhere and dragged to the bottom of the stairs to make it look like an accident."

"You may be right," Moe agreed.

"Oh, and another thing. I asked Bob Moore if he had to unlock the door to let the EMT's in. He said he did, which means that the perp couldn't have left by the front door. It has a deadbolt that has to be locked or unlocked with a key. There was no key missing. Did you notice that, Moe?"

"Chuck, I interviewed Bob Moore upstairs in our conference room. As a rule, we don't initially go the crime scene. We have crime scene technicians who know exactly what to do under any situation. They must have taken fifty shots of the family room, the living room and the position of the deceased. I think everything you've said is credible, but I still don't think the husband is a suspect, do you?"

"I'm not saying, but some of my investigation leaves a little doubt. Did you speak to Mrs. Knight, their neighbor?"

"I'm heading out there today. While I'm out that way, I'm going to stop by Bob Moore's and take a look at the door and stairs again."

"Moe, you don't mind me getting in touch with you, do you?"

"Not really, but it might be a good idea if you backed off just a little. You know how the brass is about interference with our investigations."

"A point well taken. I know what you mean."

The two men walked out together and left the parking lot at the same time. Moe headed out Bayshore Boulevard.

Log: *Met with Moe Garrett today. He thought the pictures showed the crime might have further ramifications. He did mention that I should back off a little. The investigation is going well. I feel I'm making headway.*
CCW

Who Killed Zaida Moore?

20

Moe headed out Bayshore with a plan and purpose in mind. First, he intended to interview Mrs. Estelle Knight. The second thing he was really concerned about and eager to research was the stairs, the door lock and position of the body in relation to the couch.

When he pulled into the driveway, he looked toward the garage apartment. It showed no sign of life which pleased Moe. He knew he had dispatched a jewel thief to other territories. He parked the sedan near the rear of the house and walked to the back entrance.

He rang the doorbell and it was quickly answered by Bob Moore. He was holding a book in his hand with his fingers keeping his place.

"What you reading?" Moe asked making small talk.

"It's a mystery. Pretty good too. It was written by a former Floridian."

"Who's the author?"

Bob closed the book over his finger to show the cover to Moe who read aloud, "Paid in Full" by David Shaffer. Looks interesting."

"It was a national prize winner for the writer," bragged the native Floridian.

D.E. Joyner

The two men walked through the service porch, and through the breakfast room to enter a cozy, cool sunroom. Bob invited Moe to have a seat. "Be careful, that beast on the end of the couch can't be trusted."

"What kind of dog is that?" Moe asked as he noticed the ball of fur.

"He's a Scottie, a terrier. He's the sweetest dog you ever saw. I'll tell you Moe, if I hadn't had him, I don't think I could have gotten through these past two weeks. He misses Zaida too, but he's been right by my side."

"I see your guest has left the apartment."

"Oh yes, he left Monday. I was glad to get rid of him. He said some pretty nasty things about you."

"I won't address that. Bob, the reason I'm here is that questions have been raised about the point of entry of the murderer. Can we go into the living room and let me look at the scene of the crime and evaluate it personally?"

"Sure, now things are a little messy. I haven't called the housekeeper back yet."

The two men went into the living room. Moe walked to the entrance and stood looking at the beautiful, heavy wooden door. "Is this the same lock that was on the door when the murder occurred?"

"Yes, this is the same lock that was installed when our home was being built."

"Bob, is this the door that the emergency medical team came in when you called them?"

"Yes, we seldom use this entrance. It's so much easier to park in the garage, walk to the back door, and enter through that way."

Moe turned the door handle and nothing happened. "Does it stay locked all the time?"

"Yes, we have an excellent security system, but we still keep the key to this door in a secure place."

"Where do you keep it?"

"In that urn there beside the door."

"Did you have to get the key when the EMT's came in."

"Yes."

"Had the key been moved from the place you normally leave it?"

"No, we put it in a little box that we glued inside on the side of the urn. It had not been moved."

"You returned the key to the urn when you let them in?"

"Yes, force of habit you know."

"Did the housekeeper have access to the key?" questioned Moe.

"No, she always used the back door. She had a key to use if necessary, but seldom used it because Zaida was usually home when she came to clean."

"No outsider had a key?"

"Absolutely not. You know how easy it is to get a key duplicated. We were careful that our keys didn't leave the premises."

"You're right. Now, can we assume the murderer came in through the back entrance?" Moe knew assuming anything is risky business. The thought ran through his mind the perp could have been hiding in this huge house, and never been observed.

Moe thought of all the people at the house on the day of the crime. He knew for certain the killer came in through the back door. "Bob, how well did you and Zaida know Jean Hodges?"

"She's been with us for over three years now. Zaida had a miscarriage and wasn't well for about a month. Jean worked out so well, Zaida decided to have her come twice weekly."

"Do you know anything about her background?" Moe asked.

Bob seemed to be carefully choosing his words before he spoke. "Don't think I'm a stuff shirt, but she comes from a poverty stricken background. I don't think she even finished ninth grade. She's a hard worker with a lot of good common sense."

Moe thought the same thing when he interviewed her at the housing project. "How did you and Zaida find out about Jean?"

"Zaida put an add in the newspaper and Jean answered it. We checked her criminal record and all her references. Everything checked out fine. Her references were excellent. We grew to appreciate and depend on her. Often Zaida would slip a twenty in with her check. She would stick a little Post It note on it to take Jason, her son, out to lunch on Sunday after church."

"Now Bob, how was Zaida lying when you found her?"

"She was lying on her back with one arm almost under her. The other arm was by her side."

"Was her clothing disarranged?"

"No, as I told you before, she looked like she had laid down for a nap."

"Now Bob, think. The killer used the back door for sure. It is possible he sneaked in after Jean came and hid somewhere. This house is enormous with many closets and a back stair case to get to the second floor."

"You know anything is possible, but I just don't think so. Out of habit, we all lock the back door when we come in. It's not a lock like the one on the front door, but you get used to just turning it straight up to lock it."

"Bob, tell me. Is there anything I need to know? The chief said the Spencers had hired a private investigator." Moe thought it best professionally not to tell him. He had met him and was impressed with his expertise.

"I don't know why they did that, but I'll say it's typical Preston. He's always thought money would make all things right. Actually, they instilled that philosophy in their daughter. Zaida was the kindest, sweetest woman, but she did love the dollar, or should I say she loved a bulging bank account."

"Bob, I appreciate your time. Take care of yourself and that, (what's his name) sidekick in the sunroom."

"His name's Mac. He's really a Scotsman. His full name is Mason McDougald. I call him Mac for short."

Bob walked Moe to his car and thanked him for caring so much. As he closed the door, he said, "Tell my buddy, Jim, hello, and I hope to see him soon."

D.E.Joyner

21

He left the Moore home and headed around the block to talk to Mrs. Estelle Knight. He needed no assistance to locate the address. He knew virtually every block within the city limits of Tampa. When an officer is assigned to the patrol division, he quickly learns the entire area he will be serving. With the shift change, he or she will learn a new district almost monthly.

Moe pulled into the driveway and parked the unmarked brown sedan. He walked to the front door and rang the bell. The lady of the house answered the door immediately. Moe greeted an older women he thought exuded taste and distinguished bearing. "Mrs. Knight?" he inquired.

"I'm Mrs. Estelle Knight."

"I'm Moe Garrett, a detective with the Tampa Police Department. Here's my identification," he said as he handed her his badge wallet.

"Yes, Detective Garrett, I've been expecting you for some time now, and I know what you wish to speak to me about."

"You do?" Moe asked as he tucked his wallet into his inside coat pocket. "May I ask how you know that?"

"Several days ago, a young man came to speak to me about the Moore murder. He said he had been retained by Preston Spencer."

"Was he a private investigator named Charles Wilson?"

"Yes, that's him, a real nice young man."

"I'll agree with you. Could you help him with his inquiry?"

"I don't know if I helped him or not, but he took notes about my comments," Mrs. Knight answered Moe.

"I don't want to embarrass you, but may I ask you some questions also?"

"Yes, I'll be as honest as I can," she responded.

"Mrs. Knight, did you see anyone in the Moore's yard, or around the house on the day she was killed?"

"I did see an lady exterminator spraying the yard."

"What time would you say it was?"

'I'm not sure, but I think it was a little after noon. The Price is Right had already gone off and the news was on."

"You said it was a woman. Did you see her leave the property?"

"Yes, I was upstairs and I heard the car start. I looked out the window and it was backing slowly into the part of the drive that goes under the garage apartment.. It turned and headed down the drive toward the Bayshore."

"Was there another car parked in the driveway that day?"

"I can't be sure, but the Moores have a yardman that comes on Mondays, Wednesdays and Fridays. He's been working for them for a long time now."

"Now, did you notice if he was there when the exterminator left?"

"I can't really say, but I think he was. He drives a Honda, Toyota or something like that. I think it was parked closer to the garden shed he uses. It's hard to see from upstairs. The shed hides the drive."

"Mrs. Knight, let's change gears. Did you ever see Mr. Moore in any way act physically or verbally hostile toward Mrs. Moore?"

"Detective Garrett, Mr. Moore was always the perfect gentleman. He never, to my knowledge, in any way, was hostile to his wife, physically or verbally."

"Have you observed his behavior often? I know they have a beautiful patio and garden that's visible from your home."

"Oh yes, many times. During the summer, they have guest over for cookouts. The winters are not so busy."

"Mrs. Knight, is there something you would like to tell me concerning the Zaida Moore murder?"

"You know when the other detective was here, I confided something to him. He promised me the information would never be divulged. I trusted him and took his word on the confidentiality of my interview. I see no reason to retell the sordid saga. If you'll give me a piece of paper with your printed name on it, or a piece of police department stationery, I'll write a note to Mr. Charles Wilson releasing him from his promise. I'll sign it and you can sign it. Give it to him, and he'll give the information you need."

Moe was impressed with her insight and honesty. He took a sheet of supplement stationery from his brief case and handed it to her. She went to her desk, sat down and reached for a pen in a holder. When she handed the paper back to him, he read aloud, "Mr. Charles Wilson, you have my permission to give Detective Garrett any, and all information you received during my interview. The below signature makes null and void your promise of confidentiality. Mrs. Estelle Knight."

Moe Garrett was facing a first time *permission granted* for confidential information. Pen in hand, he affixed his signature beneath Mrs. Knight's. He graciously thanked her for her very valuable information.

She assured him it was truthful in every detail. "When you see that nice Mr. Wilson, tell him I wish him well."

22

At 1400 hours Moe Garrett walked into the detective division. He was interested and could hardly wait to talk to the inspector about the interview he had with Mrs. Knight.

"Cathy, is the inspector in his office?" Moe asked.

"I think so. If he isn't, he didn't leave word on my desk pad. I just got back from lunch."

Moe walked into the inspector's office and interrupted him dozing off.

"You startled me walking in."

"Inspector, I didn't startle you, I woke you up," Moe joked.

What's on your mind, Moe?"

"This morning I interviewed a Mrs. Knight who lives directly in back of Bob and Zaida Moore. It seems she had a visit from Wilson, the PI Preston Spencer retained to further investigate Zaida's murder. She was very cooperative and impressed with his professionalism.

The thing Mrs. Knight did that affects us was to get his promise he would hold what she divulged in strictest confidence. Rather than repeat the interview, she signed a statement giving Chuck Wilson permission to relate any and everything she shared with him to me. I've never had an experience like this and don't really know where to go with it."

The inspector tapped his pencil on his desk pad. Finally he softly flipped it down and looked at Moe. "What do you think of Charles Wilson?"

"Inspector, you probably didn't know he's a former police officer. The reason for his resignation was not given. You know how the privacy laws are. Now, what do I think of him? He is one hell of a smart private investigator. He has insight into any situation. He is totally dedicated to solving the Moore murder. He is *A okay.*"

"Would you feel comfortable discussing the Knight interview with him, Moe?"

"I don't have a problem with it," Moe assured him. "I felt you should have the final say on the subject."

"Do you know how to contact him?"

"He gave me his number when we first met. Thanks Inspector, I can't wait to find out what he knows that we should know."

Moe called Chuck and they agreed to meet in the cafeteria and took a table near the back. They sat down with a cup of coffee. Sipping the coffee, Moe asked, "Chuck, would you be more comfortable if we were in a more private place?"

"Your call, if there is such a place."

"We have a room that's totally removed from noise or disruptions," Moe advised.

The two men left the half empty coffee cups and went to the room where Moe had interviewed Bob Moore. The two took their seats and Moe offered to get something for Chuck to drink.

"No thanks, I had something just before I came. That coffee was even a little much. I'm glad to meet with you again."

"Chuck, I went to Mrs. Knight's home this morning. What I thought we should discuss is something she related to me about the Moore murder investigation."

"What's that?" Chuck inquired.

"Well she signed a statement giving you permission to tell me the contents of the interview she had with you," Moe said as he removed the paper from his briefcase. He handed it to Chuck who read aloud the handwritten statement.

"Well I've never heard anything as bizarre as this, but I'll fill you in on the main points of the interview. Now Moe, this isn't verbatim, but from notes taken as she and I spoke."

"Chuck, do you mind if I take notes as we speak?"

"Take notes, write whatever I say. She released me from my confidentiality. You may not want to tell the Spencers or Bob about this discussion. I don't think it would benefit a husband or parents to know of their loved one's indiscretion."

"I won't promise I'll never tell anyone, but I'll be discreet."

Chuck looked at his notes and started to speak. "Mrs. Knight said she had seen Zaida and a man on their patio in a compromising position. She had no doubt about the identity. She has known Zaida over fifteen years. She didn't know the man, but did know the kind of car he was driving.

When I left Mrs. Knight's home, I went to the Moore's and spoke with the guest in the apartment. He reiterated her story and told me the name of Zaida's lover. He was getting ready to leave, going back to Tennessee. I thought it strange someone would cavort like that in a wide open space. When I was at the Moore home, I realized they have about a seven foot cement fence surrounding the entire backyard making it private from any onlookers."

"Chuck, can you give me the name of the victim's lover?"

"Sorry, I can't do that. I promised him his name would never be told. I can tell you this, he is in no way involved in the murder. His alibi is air tight. I even checked out his wife. They are a loving family who don't need to have their marriage damaged by this type of trouble. Do you feel the same way I do?"

"You're right, Chuck. If you're sure he is not involved, we'll forget about the indiscretion. I don't think the innocent unknown lover will change the investigation." Moe did reflect on the interview he had with Bob Moore. He knew it was possible for spouses to have affairs without changing their status in anyway.

"Moe I'm sure about it. As a suspect, he's clean. I even checked on his wife's whereabouts on the day of the crime. She volunteered at their son's school. She was in the classroom at least two hours. You know schools appreciate their volunteers and keep records of regarding the hours they worked."

"Chuck, sounds to me like you've covered all the bases. I'm not putting your info in a supplement, but I have made notes and they'll be retained in my personal file. Man, I thank you for your help. Sounds like you were a policeman once."

"You know damned well I was. Maybe I wasn't at the top of the heap, but I did the best I could."

Moe and Chuck shook hands as he left the detective division. Then Moe walked to the inspector's office. He caught him wide awake. "Well Moe, what did you find out?"

"Inspector, I think Chuck is one sharp cookie. I respect him more each time our paths cross. I took notes, but I'm not putting them in the report. I have them in my personal file if you need them."

23

Within three days the lab had returned the completed examination of the whetstone. The test was more thorough than Detective Garrett had expected. It seemed that the prints were almost etched in the surface. Since oil is used on a whetstone, they were easy for the lab to lift. Also, there was a small smear of blood on the whetstone. The blood type was "A negative." Detective Garrett quickly checked the prints with the I.D. tech on duty. They were identical to those of Freddie Barnes. This fact didn't surprise Garrett. He knew that Freddie used the stone two and sometimes three times weekly. What did surprise him was the smear of blood.

Detective Garrett called Freddie and asked him if he knew his blood type. He said that his blood type was "O positive." Moe knew that African Americans rarely have a negative Rh. factor. This raised an immediate question. Whose blood was on the whetstone?

He called Doctor Sheppard and asked about Zaida Moore's blood type. He could give no information, but said to give him thirty minutes and he'd have the answer. For Detective Garrett that thirty minutes seemed like thirty hours. When his phone rang, he caught it before it had time to ring twice.

"Moe Garrett here."

"That was fast. Moe, I have the info that you requested. You probably didn't know that Zaida Moore had a miscarriage three and a half years ago. I called the hospital and they had her blood type available. Her doctor almost lost her, and a transfusion was necessary. Her blood type is "A negative." It's not the most common type, but not rare either."

"I can't thank you enough, Doc. If you ever need a police officer, I'm your man. Yes, you too," Garret responded as the doctor said to have a nice day.

For Morris Daniel Garrett, this would be a red letter day in his homicide career.

Inspector Bridges was in his office when Moe walked into the detective division. He had left word with his secretary to tell Moe he needed to see him as soon as he came in. Garrett dropped his briefcase beside a chair and slumped over and slid into the seat across from Inspector Bridges.

"How are things going, Moe?"

"Everything is good, that is, as good as could be expected, Inspector."

"What do you mean by that?"

"We may have a break in the Zaida Moore case."

"Since when?"

"Well, this morning the test came back on the possible murder weapon. I was coming in to speak to you about it. You'll get a copy of the supplement. Gonzalez was copying it when I was in records. He'll probably hand deliver it before lunch. I know he won't use the pneumatic tube for this supplemental report."

"Fill me in on the details."

"You know the Moores have a yardman that works Mondays, Wednesdays and Fridays. Well, it seems that he could be the killer. The murder weapon is a whetstone. It had the suspect's fingerprints on it. They have been identified as those belonging to one Freddie Eli Barnes, B/M, DOB 16 December 65."

Who Killed Zaida Moore?

"That name doesn't ring a bell."

"No, he doesn't have much of a rap sheet. A couple of misdemeanors and a grand theft that was dismissed. Listen, his prints would have been on a garden tool since he's a gardener, but a smear of blood matches that of Zaida Moore. There's no question, our lab makes few mistakes. Also, the autopsy report said the blunt force trauma was caused by a heavy square object.

"Garrett, I know you have worked on the case long and hard. A commendation is sure to come your way."

"No accolades needed, Inspector, it's all in a day's work. Now, when and how shall we make the arrest?"

"Okay, here's what we'll do. Tomorrow is Wednesday. Freddie leaves for work at about 0645 hours. I'll assign Mike Thatcher to go with you. Also, I'll call Inspector Garcia and have him assign one of his men. I know you could handle this by yourself, but we're taking no chances. Don't forget your Miranda and be sure that you make Barnes aware of all his rights, especially his right to legal counsel. Moe, you know how many good cases have ended in mistrials or nolle prossed because of an officer's failure to advise the defendant of his rights. Plan to meet at the station at 0530 hours."

Sleep wasn't in the cards that night for Moe Garrett. He would doze off, wake up, sit on the side of the bed, lie down, doze off, and wake up. Finally, about four o'clock, he got up and put the coffee on. While the coffee was brewing, he got into the shower, dried himself briskly and dressed for the day. He poured himself a cup of coffee and looked up at the wall clock. It was ten 'til five and almost time to leave to make an arrest that he knew would change a lot of people's lives. He had thought Freddie and Grace were poor, but honest and loving. "Oh well, such is life," he thought aloud.

At 0500 hours there wasn't much traffic so Detective Garrett made the drive to the station in fifteen minutes. He entered an empty cafeteria and took a seat. In a minute Officer Ed Kelly came in and sat down with him. "What's up, man?"

"Did Inspector Garcia tell you that you are going out to make an arrest?"

"No, he said that you would fill me in on all the details."

"We'll wait until Detective Thatcher comes in and then we'll discuss our plan and details. We'll all have a say in the strategy we'll use."

As he finished the sentence, Thatcher walked through the door.

"Hey, Bud," he greeted his co-worker and friend.

"Okay, here's what we'll do. Detective Thatcher and I will take the unmarked. Officer Kelly, you take the squad car. I'm sure one reason the inspector picked you was because of the retainer in back of the front seat. The address we're going to is 411, 31st Street, Apartment No. 8 upstairs. We'll all get there at the same time. Ed, you draw your weapon and go around to the back of the building. Mike, you and I will go to the front door. Wait a minute for Ed to get to the back, and then go into the building and up the stairs. We'll knock on the door and wait for an answer. Are we all on the same page?"

"Yes." both men replied.

"Let's go, men."

Little was said by Garrett or Thatcher. They drove the approximately three miles in almost complete silence. There was no need for conversation since each knew the plan.

No car was parked in front of 411, so both police vehicles had ample room. Moe Garrett parked first, followed by Ed Kelly. They observed that no one was stirring in the neighborhood. Being in early spring, it was still just breaking day when the three men approached the front of the apartment building. Officer Kelly cut to the left and hurried around the building. Detectives Garrett and Thatcher walked into the building and quietly waited a little while. Then they climbed the stairs and stopped in front of apartment 8. Detective Garrett knocked three times on the door.

"Who is it?" a half asleep man called out.

"Tampa Police Department, Detective Garrett."

"What you want at this time of day?"

"We need to talk to you."

"Bout what?"

"Open the door, Freddie Eli Barnes."

Freddie opened the door and stood wearing only boxer shorts. Moe wouldn't have recognized him as he was wearing a stocking cap on his head.

"Freddie Eli Barnes, you are under arrest for the murder of one Zaida Ellen Moore. Be advised that you are entitled to legal counsel and that you may remain silent. If you understand what I have said, answer me at this time."

"Yes, I understand you, but I don't understand why."

"Anything that you say may be used against you in a court of law. Do you completely understand what I have said?"

"Yes, I understand."

"No other comment need be made," Moe Garrett replied.

There was no reason for a search or pat-down since Freddie was undressed. Officer Kelly and Detective Thatcher stood within arms reach as Freddie slipped on khakis and a tee shirt. He brought a pair of socks and shoes into the living room and sat in a chair to put them on. He ripped the cap from his head and smoothed his hair down.

Grace who had been awakened by the commotion walked out of the bedroom carrying baby, Carinda. "What's all this about?" she cried.

"It's all right baby, I'm sure there's been a mistake. Take care of Carinda."

Detective Thatcher snapped a pair of handcuffs on Freddie's wrists in back of him. Without another word, he was put into the patrol car. The door automatically locking. Garrett and Thatcher followed the prisoner and Officer Kelly to the booking section. Two guards were waiting in the booking bay to take Freddie from the car into the booking section.

Little was said as the booking process was initiated. Freddie was treated kindly and courteously. The prisoner was taken into an area where he was stripped down and given jail clothing to wear. He was placed in a holding area until he could be taken before the magistrate to be formally charged with the murder of Zaida Ellen Moore.

Early the next morning, after Freddie had spent nearly a full day in the holding area, drinking weak coffee and eating bologna sandwiches made on stale bread, he had a visitor. Moe Garrett had him brought into a visiting room. "Ready to talk, Freddie?"

"Detective Garrett, I'm not guilty. Please believe me."

"Yeah, yeah, neither was Ted Bundy."

"I don't have nothing to say."

"I want to give you an opportunity to sign a confession. If you do, the judge will most likely go easier on you."

"Man, I can't say I did it when I didn't."

"Okay, I'll see you later," Moe said as he closed his briefcase and walked out the door.

Who Killed Zaida Moore?

24

Excitement ran pretty high in the detective division for several reasons. Number one, the Moore murder being solved. Number two, several men in the detective division had taken the test for sergeant and every single one had passed. There were five on the list which was active for an indeterminate amount of time. Detective Garrett was on the list. He knew that all five men couldn't remain in the detective division, but would be assigned to patrol, traffic, services, vice or crime prevention. He had been in the division for over three years and wanted to stay put.

Number three, most citizens weren't aware of the F.B.I. Report on Crime Statistics. A monthly report is sent to the Bureau with all crimes and arrests reported. A police department lives or dies with the monthly report. Even though the public doesn't know the in's and out's of the reporting, a negative headline in the local paper will bring the wrath of the city fathers down on the police department. For six months the arrest record had been phenomenal. Enough good things could not be said about the effectiveness of the local department.

As a show of appreciation, free dinners were given to the men and their families by several leading local restaurants. The Ringling Bros., Barnum and Bailey Circus was making its annual Tampa appearance, and had passed out more free tickets than one could imagine. This was a two-fold benefit. Positively enhanced were public safety and relations. The money spent on food and trinkets was incredible. One police officer and spouse, or whomever, with an average of two children, could leave some big bucks under the big top.

Back to the list for sergeant. The increase in pay wasn't substantial, but if an officer wanted to move on up, he or she had to become a sergeant. The rank of corporal was also available and more easily achieved. All divisions had ranked personnel, but the greatest need was naturally in the traffic and patrol divisions. Most men who joined the police department planned to be career law enforcement officers and thought about eventual retirement. Rank enhanced the retirement income.

It had been almost two days since Freddie Barnes had been arrested. Under the sixth amendment, all arrested persons are entitled to appear before a magistrate quickly. Also, if indigent, they must be given legal representation. Usually a poor person is assigned counsel according to a list that the presiding Superior Court Judge's office maintains. This process might be slightly flawed, but it's almost nationwide.

Freddie Barnes was indigent, therefore was assigned a lawyer. His counsel was a young white woman in her mid-twenties namned Lisa Swanson. She had recently passed the state bar examination. Lisa was rather plain, but very well groomed. Her speech and delivery were dynamic.

She had been in touch with Freddie's common law wife. Her advice was to bring the best clothes that Freddie owned to the city jail for his first court appearance. She personally paid for a hair style, since she thought his Afro was a little much.

Who Killed Zaida Moore?

On day three Freddie was transported to the county court house. He was confined to a holding area. He hadn't seen Detective Garrett, but knew he would be there when needed. Also, he hadn't seen Grace, but was permitted to speak to her on the phone.

Brought into the courtroom by a guard, Freddie was instructed to sit on the second row. Waiting for him was Lisa Swanson. He spotted Grace near the back of the room. Her face showed that she had been under a lot of stress. She didn't have Carinda, and Freddie thought she probably had left her with her mother.

Freddie did look sharp in a tan double-breasted suit. A brown, rather wide tie with maroon designs ran down his white shirt.

"Will the defendant Freddie Eli Barnes please stand."

Freddie stood and looked straight ahead at the magistrate.

" Mr. Barnes, you are charged with capital murder in the death of one Zaida Ellen Moore. How do you plead?"

"Not guilty, your honor."

"Very well, will the arresting officer please take the stand. You may sit down Mr. Barnes."

Detective Garrett stood and held a manila folder in front of him.

"Will you please give the court your name, rank and the agency you represent."

"I am Detective Morris Daniel Garrett. I represent the Tampa Police Department, County of Hillsborough, State of Florida."

"State the charges against the defendant Freddie Eli Barnes."

"Your Honor, the defendant Freddie Eli Barnes is charged with capital murder, the victim being one Zaida Ellen Moore."

"On what evidence do you base this charge?"

"Overwhelming evidence, your honor. The defendant, a gardener at the victim's home, was present on the day of the murder. He has admitted being in the kitchen that day. Also, the possible murder weapon with the defendant's fingerprints on it is secured in the property room at the Tampa Police Department. Evidence number D.H.10677. When we sent the weapon to the lab, a smear of blood was identified on it."

"Whose blood?"

"It was the same blood type as Zaida Ellen Moore's. She died from blunt force trauma to the back of the head. Her injury, according to Doctor Kenneth W. Sheppard, the pathologist, was extreme trauma to the autonomic nervous system. She lost little blood as a result of the injury. Also, the doctor stated that if you were struck on the arm with the same force as the victim's head injury, it would probably have left a nasty bruise, but little else. The brain in the affected area can't stand much force applied to it."

"Well explained," the judge complimented.

Lisa Swanson showed no emotion, nor did she offer to speak out. She looked at her client and at Detective Garrett.

"Ms. Swanson, welcome to the court. I don't believe we've met before. How does your client plead?"

Lisa Swanson had a very distinguished appearance reaching for her briefcase and slowly stood. "Thank you, your honor. My client pleads not guilty. I must take issue with two things that I've been made aware of. Blood evidence is not admissible in a court of law without further and extreme testing. Also, my client was advised that he would be given a polygraph examination. It has not been given yet."

Who Killed Zaida Moore?

The magistrat spoke clearly and forcefully, "I don't have Detective Garrett's expertise on various evidential presentations, but I do know that your client is entitled to a polygraph to be given immediately. The charge of capital murder will stand. No bond will be allowed. I remand the defendant to the Hillsborough County Jail. A court date will be set as soon as possible."

Detective Moe Garrett knew that blood samples weren't admissible in court, but he thought that mentioning the blood type would have a positive effect on the case. He also had to admire and respect the young lawyer who had presented Freddie's case with such knowledge and authority.

Moe left the courthouse and went straight to see Inspector Bridges. The inspector was in his office and invited Moe to come in.

"Inspector, can we give Freddie Barnes a polygraph as soon as possible?"

"Certainly, I'll call Sheriff Brantley and have him brought over today. You know that we have one of the best operators in the state. His results are rarely challenged. I'll call to make arrangements for his services today if possible." Moe waited until Inspector Bridges finished his telephone conversation. "It's all set up. The test will be given at the county jail. They have a facility that's almost as good as ours. I'll take the report over myself and after he's made his notes, I'll bring it back. We should have the results before we leave today."

"Inspector, I do appreciate your help in this matter."

It had been several days since Moe had taken time to look over the offenses assigned to him before and after the Moore case. He went into his office and pulled the reports from his file. There was really nothing that needed his immediate attention.

Moe hadn't been too excited about things lately. He attributed it to his being so wrong about the guilt of Freddie Barnes. He was certain that was the reason he overlooked the polygraph. Well, that mistake was in the correction box. At 1130 hours Moe decided to go for an early lunch. He and the Inspector returned at the same time. "Come on in Moe, I have the polygraph and summation results."

"Well?"

"It's inconclusive, but some areas showed that he was lying. When asked if he had ever touched Zaida Moore, he said no. The machine went crazy. The polygraph isn't good evidence, not admissible in court anyway, but you may want to keep it handy for leverage. The operator cooperated with us. He quickly got it ready while I waited. I thanked Sheriff Brantley. He's a good man, Moe."

"I'll agree with that, after all he is one of our own."

Moe left the department behind at 1700 hours. He collected Lou Ann and Mary Beth and headed for Clearwater Beach. He needed some down time and the beach always provided it. On the way, they stopped at Mary Beth's favorite place and picked up a Happy Meal and two combos. The next stop was the beach. They watched Mary Beth chase fiddler crabs and feed most of her sandwich to a huge flock of seagulls.

Sundown found the Garrett family tired but stress free after the salt air and spray removed the strain from their bodies. After Mary Beth was bathed and put to bed, Lou Ann curled up beside her man and whispered, "How about some baby making practice, Love."

Moe was amused and answered his adoring wife, "Tonight Honey, a promise is about as good as a performance."

25

One of Moe's coworkers and friends in homicide was a very smart African American detective named Hank Crandell. Not only did he have the respect of the black community, but he had the total respect of the Tampa Police Department. He had solved more cases than any detective on the force.

Very often Crandell and Garrett would meet for coffee at a small café near the police department. This morning was a meeting time for the twosome. They met, touched knuckles and chose a booth near the back of the café.

"Congratulations on solving the Moore case," Hank said.

"You know Hank, I'm glad to solve the case. The evidence was there definitely, but I feel bad for that family. I do."

"Well, it just happens I know the family."

"How do you know them?"

"I don't really know much about Freddie, but their mother and I went all through school together. She was actually still in high school when the twins were born. Probably not more than about sixteen or seventeen years old at the time of their birth When they were small, they were the cutest little guys you ever saw. Freddie was very light, or bright complexioned. Mary was darker. Their proud mother always brought them to

Sunday school and church. They were dressed in their best and one sat on one side of mom and one on the other. I always felt she was a good mother who tried to bring her little ones up right."

"Was there a father in the home?"

"There may have been one at home. I'm not sure, but I never saw one at church with them. You see, Moe, I left the area to go to college in Tallahassee and never really returned there."

"I didn't know you ever lived on the east side."

"Thirty to forty years ago almost all blacks lived on the east side. There were a few pockets in other areas, but not enough to hardly count. A few lived in what used to be Port Tampa. They mostly worked at the docks which were active at that time."

"How old are you, Hank?"

"I'll be forty-two soon."

"Man, you sure don't look it."

"We don't show our age and you can't tell us apart either."

"You sucker!" Both enjoyed a good laugh over Hank's racial comments.

"What's happening with you since the last time we met, Hank?"

"You really don't want to know."

"Lay it on me."

"Well, I've worked on two rapes, both unfounded. Moe I get so sick of working long and hard on a case and it not amounting to anything."

"Did the victims just decide that they couldn't go through with the case? They're bad sometimes and the victim is actually treated like a criminal, or vilified."

"No, one of the complainants, notice I didn't use victim, was mad because her John didn't want to pay her the ten spot he promised. He said it wasn't worth but two dollars. He threw the two bucks on the chest of drawers and walked out. She really was upset and yelled rape. I knew her background and told her she could be arrested for filing a false crime report. She immediately changed her story and was ready to vacate the premises pronto."

"Hank, that's so funny you ought to send it to Hustler. How about number two?"

"That's even better. The complainant might have had a little force used, but during her interview, she showed a great deal of excitement. Finally, I asked her if she had sketted? You know what that means, don't you?"

"Hank, you know I know what sket means."

"Well, her answer really knocked me back.. What she said was 'Only twice.' Moe can you imagine that?"

"No, but I surely would like to meet that lady." The stories were funny, even though a little sad, and both detectives enjoyed the humor.

"Moe, have you a tale to tell?"

"None as good as yours. I did have something happen last week that I thought was funny."

"Well, go for it."

"You knew I was married before I married Lou Ann, didn't you?"

"Yes, I think you told me, maybe two or three times."

"Last week I was waiting at a club to meet a snitch. You know I was assigned that drug related murder last week."

"Yes, I knew and I figured you'd soon solve it."

"I was sitting having a drink and looked across the room. It must have been girl's night out, as half a dozen good looking women were enjoying a drink. I surveyed them and one beauty looked familiar. When she walked toward me, I thought, 'that's Stacey.' She parked herself at my table and dropped a business card with her address written and circled."

She said, "My husband's out of town. Drop by for old times sake."

"I hadn't seen her in years and was stunned by what happened. It didn't take me long to construct the picture and respond. I said, you know Stacey when we were eighteen, I thought you were the only girl that had what I couldn't get enough of. Now, I know every woman has one. Lou Ann, my wife, has the best, and the best thing is no one taps it but me. 'Thanks, but no thanks' I said as I handed the card back to her"

She said, "You bastard."

"When she got back to her table, she stuck her middle finger up at me. Can you believe that? I raised my glass and acknowledged her with a salute. She was livid, grabbed her purse and left the scene."

"Moe, that's like a television show."

"It happened, Boss."

"Let's cut out Moe, duty calls."

The two men got into their cars and headed in different directions to perform their sworn duties.

Who Killed Zaida Moore?

26

Being the father of four children is sometimes an overwhelming experience. You have to be organized to fit in all their activities. Jim Donavan was such a father. His two sons, his oldest children, played baseball. During the baseball season, they either were at practice or playing almost every evening. They were good kids and their dad was proud of them. He helped coach their teams when time permitted. The girls were very athletic also. They couldn't wait to join a big girl's softball team.

You know the old saying, 'If you want a job done, ask a person who is already busy.' Donavan had a plate running over when asked if he would help organize a Police Department Ladies Slow Pitch Softball team.

He readily agreed and the team became a reality. The ladies were fair players, winning almost as many as they lost. The games were enjoyed by husbands and kids who came out to watch mom play. The team existed for almost two years. After that, interest waned, and the team disbanded.

It occurred to Jim one day after Zaida Moore had been dead almost a month that he had been so busy he hadn't seen Bob Moore. He called Bob and invited him to lunch. He felt it would do him good to get out. He didn't think Bob had gone back to his office, but that was no big deal. His father was still quite active. Even though he was close to seventy years old,

Bob's father kept his hand in the lucrative business. Jim and Bob were to meet at a favorite restaurant on the Causeway. Bob arrived first and was drinking a martini when Jim pulled into the parking lot. The friends hugged and Jim ordered a glass of iced tea.

"You can handle something stronger than that can't you Jim?"

"I'm the designated driver today. I don't touch the stuff during working hours," Jim explained.

"Don't mind if I do, do you?"

"No, but be careful. I don't want you to become a statistic."

The two men ordered lunch and settled into conversation.

"Jim, it's been nearly a month since Zaida died. I'm barely coping."

"Things will get better. You know it takes time to heal a broken heart caused by the death of a loved one," his friend advised.

I've had time to reflect on my life for the past month. You know Jim, we were married for almost twelve years."

"I know, I was your best man, remember?"

"How could I forget? That was one hell of a bachelor party."

"What are you talking about?" Jim jokingly inquired.

"The booze, the girls, and finally breakfast at 5:00 a.m. at an all night restaurant for the bachelor party. We must have been a sad looking lot by that hour. I got up to use the bathroom about the same time our food arrived. Remember what you did?"

Donavan couldn't contain his laughter. "All I did was sprinkle a little saltpeter on your scrambled eggs. Not enough to hurt you, just enough to keep you from being so horny."

"You dog, but it didn't work, so the joke's on you." Bob raised his glass to order another martini.

It was served and he took a huge swallow. For some drinkers, alcohol incurs silence, for others it seems to loosen the tongue to a great extent. Bob Moore could be placed in the later category. By the time he'd consumed the second martini, his tongue was well oiled.

"You're my best friend, Jim. You're the only one left I can talk man to man with."

"I feel the same way Bob. We are kinda like David and Jonathan," Jim mused.

"Sure it's not like David and Goliath?" the near drunk asked.

"Man, you don't know your Bible."

"Jim, let's get serious. There're things I want to tell you. Not that it matters now, but I have to talk to somebody."

"Shoot."

"You know that Zaida and I had a wonderful marriage, that was until about three and a half years ago. After she lost our little boy, she changed. It was almost as if she blamed me for the miscarriage. I tried to comfort her, but it didn't work. She only seemed to get comfort from the bottle. She drank every day. By the time I got home, she was usually drunk. Our sex life was non-existent. I could handle that, if you know what I mean."

"I understand completely. You know Dot and I have four kids."

"Okay, the thing that Zaida did that I couldn't handle was her constantly berating me in front of our friends, or even sometimes total strangers. About two months ago we went to the country club for dinner. There were four couples at our table. I knew two of the men and their wives. As a matter of fact, one of the men was an alumnus of Georgia Tech. Zaida struck up a conversation with him. She dumbfounded all at the table with the following remarks."

'Dennis, you're an alumni of Georgia Tech, right?'

'Yes, and proud of it,' he responded nodding at me.

'Know what course they should offer there?'

'What do you think they should offer?'

Zaida loudly proclaimed, 'Screwing 101. Anyway, that's what Bob needed.'

"Jim, I was so embarrassed. I couldn't think of a retort. There were a few snickers, but you could tell our table, and our dinner, became very uncomfortable for the rest of the evening."

"What you should have said was, 'I don't seem to have trouble with my other partners.' That would have shut her up."

"Jim, you know I've always been rather quiet. I'm just not quick with repartee. Also, I suspect that Zaida was being intimate with other men. I couldn't prove it, but the evidence was there, even Mark Pierce."

"I'm shocked, Bob, I never would have thought she would be that type."

"You don't know until you live with someone, do you?"

"You've got that right." Captain Donavan thought back to Detective Garrett's interview with the gardener. Could his account of the incident have been true?

"Don't mention our conversation. It's not something I'm proud of. If this were to get out, our parents would be heartbroken. You see, my parents are in deep grief over the loss of Zaida. Her parents both have had to be counseled by their minister. You know she was their only child."

Jim looked at the empty martini glass. "Okay big guy, it's coffee time. Order it black, one for here and one for the road. You know I've never approved of a two martini lunch."

Who Killed Zaida Moore?

"I really needed this, Jim. You know I've been down lately. Maybe now I can get on with my life, return to work and not dwell on the past so much."

"Bob, let's go fishing, just the two of us down to the Keys. The weather's perfect now."

"We'll see about it. Oh, I almost forgot, I picked up Zaida's rings from the property room. Jim, just looking at those rings tore me apart. I gave one of them to her when we got engaged. I was young and not very smart about money. It took me two years to pay for that ring. I guess she enjoyed wearing it. I stopped by your office, but you had left early for a doctor's appointment. Many thanks pal."

"See you later good buddy. Be careful going home."

Captain Donavan headed back to the station to complete his tour of duty. He thought of the many times when he was younger, he wished to be in the position of his friend. He was good looking, educated, healthy and wealthy. All the things that people wish for. At the moment, he was grateful for the little things in life that made him so happy.

When he entered his office, he took a cigar from his desk, prepared it in the usual way, lit it and blew a puff of smoke into a ring. Yes, even his cigar was counted as one of his many blessings.

He picked up his phone and dialed Inspector Bridges' extension. His secretary answered. "How is the prettiest gal in the detective division?"

"Captain, you say that to all the girls. If I'm so pretty, why am I still ringless?" said Cathy, the clerk typist in the detective division.

"You just won't settle for anything but the best, young lady. Your day will come, believe me. Say, is that boss of yours available ?"

"He just stepped out, said he would be in the cafeteria."

"Thanks, I'll catch him in the hall." Captain Donavan, cigar in hand, walked out into the hall just as the Inspector walked into the cafeteria. He got his coffee and sat down at a table along the wall. As he sat, Captain Donavan pulled out a chair at the same table and sat down.

"I need to talk to you, Inspector. I had lunch with Bob Moore today. The man's a wreck. I'm not sure he can handle losing Zaida."

"You know that time will help. Did he mention anything about the man that killed Zaida?"

"Not one word. He did say that Zaida hadn't been well lately. Not physically but emotionally. I tried to talk to him about the two of us maybe going fishing down at the Keys. Get his mind off things."

"What did he say to that?"

"Not much, I don't think much is sinking in now."

"You know Jim, my father lost my mother when I was almost fifteen. She was forty-six. Died suddenly with a massive cerebral hemorrhage" My twenty-year-old sister and I thought we would have to bury Dad too. He cried every evening about sundown. It was almost unbearable to watch. It took him six months to begin to even act alive. When mother had been dead eighteen months, he married the widow of one of his friends who had been dead for five years. They're still married, both in their late seventies. Look, Bob will survive, believe me."

After an exchange of small talk, both men returned to their offices. Another day had transpired with nothing significant happening at the police department. As they say, "No news is good news" is always true at the police department, which deals twenty-four-seven with all of life's tragedies.

27

Lisa Swanson had spoken with Barnes three times since he was incarcerated. At her last interview, she spoke quite frankly with her client.

"Freddie, tell me. Did you kill Zaida Moore? You know it won't matter; you're still entitled to legal counsel. We'll just take a different approach when you go to trial. Now, did you kill the lady?"

"Honest, Miss Lisa, I did not kill Zaida Moore. I've never killed anybody. I won't even wring a chicken's neck. I'm a peace-loving man."

"I believe you Freddie."

"Thanks, Miss Lisa."

"I want you to think back. Was there ever any way at anytime that Zaida's blood could have gotten on that whetstone? Now think."

Later that day Lisa Swanson came to the police department. She went to the detective division to speak with Moe Garrett. Inspector Bridges spoke with her since Garrett was not in. He had communications raise him and a meeting was arranged.

It may seem that the police and the defense lawyer would be on opposite sides and find it rather difficult to communicate. As a civil servant, it's wise to be aware that politics makes strange bed fellows. You may be talking to a foe who could be your boss next month. Civil Service is fair in testing and giving assignments. As a person gains professional stature he could be elected a judge, commissioner or even mayor.

During one election a well-known municipal judge wasn't up for re-election, but a man with his same name paid his entry fee and entered the race for a councilman. Even though he was totally unqualified for the post, he won handily. Name recognition is, and always has been, a valuable asset to one seeking election.

Moe and Lisa Swanson met at the parking lot of a bank. Moe got out of the unmarked car and got into Lisa's compact car and thanked her for her concern and promptness.

Lisa responded, "Thank you for meeting me, Detective Garrett. Now, let's get to the point. Yesterday, Freddie Barnes requested and was granted a meeting with me. At the interview, he recalled something that happened several days before Zaida Moore was murdered. Here is how he remembers the incident.

Mrs. Moore was out beside the rose garden when he was cutting the roses. She admired a beautiful, but very thorny deep red Chrysler Imperial rose that he had cut. She reached for it and a heavy thorn stuck her right middle finger. Naturally, it bled profusely. Freddie had a Kleenex in his pocket. He quickly held the tissue on the wound. When it stopped bleeding, the tissue, dampened with blood, was put into his pocket to discard later. That same pocket held the whetstone. My client thinks Mrs. Moore's blood was smeared on the whetstone at that time. Detective Garrett, this is a feasible reason for the blood evidence, don't you think? You know that the polygraph went crazy when he was asked if he had ever touched Mrs. Moore. This incident could have caused that also."

A smart, thoughtful Moe responded, "You know you could be right. Why don't you bring this incident out at the trial."

"Trial, hell. Before it starts, I'm going before the judge to have it dismissed for lack of evidence."

Detective Garrett knew if he ever needed an attorney, he was looking at a damned good one, a smart one, one without balls, but plenty of guts. It was necessary for Moe not to tip his hand since there was no positive proof that Freddie was telling the truth, or that he wasn't the guilty party. Moe knew that anything could cause a judge to throw out an indictment, especially if the police report or evidence had even a tiny flaw. He had certainly witnessed it before. Then the case was back to square one.

"By the way Detective Garrett, did you know Preston Spencer had hired a private investigator from the Jacksonville area?"

"Yes," Moe acknowledged. "I think they hired him about five days after the murder. I've met the gent. I think he's a well intentioned investigator. How and when did you find about him?"

"As Freddie attorney, I'm concerned that he was not given every benefit of doubt that should have preceded his arrest. Because of my feelings, I visited the rose garden. I spoke with the victim's husband who gave me permission to survey the entire area. Bob Moore came out and chatted with me as we walked. He was totally surprised with the arrest of Freddie. He gave me the name and phone number of Charles Wilson. Naturally I wanted an interview with him. Before I contacted him, I contacted the DA's office to make sure no rules about interviewing a privately hired investigator would be abridged. The DA's office said it was all right, so I called him."

"What did you think after talking with him?"

"I thought Zaida's father would dismiss him after an arrest was made. He said he had signed a contract with Preston Spencer. Even if an arrest was made, he was still under contract. Because of this, he continued to interview people. Also, he had a personal interest in the case."

Moe asked for his own information, "What did you think about his professionalism?"

"He seemed to be very methodical in his investigation. He made no comment about the arrest. I did get the feeling he wasn't totally pleased with the value of the evidence. He had nothing negative to say about the department."

"You know he was in law enforcement in Jacksonville."

"Actually, he did mention his prior experience in law enforcement."

"Ms. Swanson, is there anything else we should discuss? If not, I'd better be getting back to my assignment." Moe opened the door and without looking back approached the brown unmarked, opened the door and headed away from the parking lot.

Lisa Swanson, who had no chance to respond, had a rather dejected feeling as Moe walked to the unmarked. She couldn't help but consider him a cocky shit-head. No doubt, he was a good detective, but his inability to have anything but tunnel vision was cause for concern. She decided to contact Chuck Wilson to get his take on the arrest and the blood evidence unrelated to the crime according to the accused murderer.

She dialed his number after retrieving it from many papers and cards stored at random in the console. When he answered, she was just a little hesitant to start a conversation.

"You may not remember me, but I'm Lisa Swanson, the attorney assigned to represent Freddie Barnes who's charged with the murder of Zaida Moore.

"Ms. Swanson, I do remember you. We discussed the case on the phone. I believe it's been nearly a week ago now."

"That's right Mr. Wilson. Something's come up that I need your opinion on."

"Ms. Swanson, in what part of town do you live?"

"I live just south of Bay to Bay off Dale Mabry. Do you know the area?"

"I think I know about where you're located. It's nearly time for me to call it a day. Would you like to meet me for dinner? We can discuss the case then."

"But we've never met, how will I know you?" Lisa asked rather excitedly.

"Okay, I'm a pretty regular looking joe. I have dark hair and am about six feet tall. To add a little intrigue, when you think you know which man I am, walk up to me and say 'you fly'? If I answer, 'only if the rigging is tight', you'll know you have the right man. Got that in your head?"

Lisa thought and replied, "I think so. I just have to remember two words."

"Let's meet at Denny's on Dale Mabry. Is the time six-thirty all right with you?"

"Fine, that'll give me time to run home and change into something more casual."

Lisa was a little excited to be going on a blind diner date with a man she'd only spoken to on the phone. Her schedule had been so hectic with three cases, she'd had little time for any recreation.

She dressed with care and sprayed a little perfume on her wrists and behind her ears. She carefully arranged her hair. All finished, she surveyed herself in the mirror in the corner of her bedroom. Everything met with her approval. She left her apartment at six-fifteen and headed north on Dale Mabry.

Even though Denny's was busy, she found a parking place right in front. When she approached the entrance, she noticed a good-looking man standing beside the door. She took a deep breath, walked up to him and timidly asked, "You fly?"

The man showed at least twenty-four teeth as he replied, "Where you want to fly to, baby?"

Lisa turned ten shades of red as she flipped away from the stranger. She didn't think the whole idea was brilliant. As she entered the restaurant, she noticed a man seated at the front on a bench. She walked up to him and gathered the courage to get out the two words "You fly?"

"Only if the rigging is tight," he replied.

"I'm Lisa," she said between outbursts of laughter.

"I'm Chuck. It's so good to meet you in person."

"Chuck, see that man over there, the one sitting down now with the blond lady. I asked him if he flew. I think he thought I flew from the mental ward at the hospital."

"Now Lisa, our dinner has to be great. It started on a high note. Agree?"

"Surely," Lisa nodded as she looked her blind date over without being so obvious. "I haven't eaten here before, have you?"

"Oh yes. This isn't too far from my apartment. I can tell you the food is good, especially the breakfast."

"Have you had the shepherd's pie?" she asked.

"Not here, but I've eaten it before at other restaurants."

"What kind of pie is it?"

"It's not a pie like pumpkin. It's a meat dish. Kind of like hamburger, mashed potatoes and gravy in a baking dish."

"Sounds good to me."

Who Killed Zaida Moore?

Looking the menu over, Chuck decided on Salisbury steak, a baked potato and a salad. "You know I have to watch my calories."

The salad arrived and allowed Lisa, who was not very verbal with the handsome stranger, something to say. "Good looking salad, Chuck. The dressing looks good too."

"It does look good. A salad is one thing I can make that tastes good. They always turn exactly as I want them."

"Do you do your own cooking?"

"I do. I haven't found anyone to take the job off my hands yet."

"Chuck, are you married?" Lisa asked hoping the answer would be in the negative.

"I was, but I'm divorced and have been for five years. I also have a seven year old son. What's your status?"

"Single, at this time. I don't even have a man in my life, period. I really have been too busy to include a personal relationship in my schedule. I worked my way through law school and passed the bar six months ago. You know it's not easy working and attending law school."

"I know. Where did you grow up, Lisa?"

"I was born in Germany. My dad was in the Air Force. He was stationed at Mac Dill before he retired. We liked the area, so we decided to settle here. I graduated from Stetson Law School. Where are your roots?"

"Not just my roots, but the whole tree is from Jacksonville. As far as I know, we've been there for five generations. So much for our genealogy. Lisa, what did you want to discuss with me about the Zaida Moore case?"

"I've talked to the arrested murderer, Freddie Barnes, and I feel there are just too many holes in the case to suit me," Lisa said in a tone of voice that was measured and to the point.

"I don't know about that, but I do know the evidence was almost foolproof. Moe Garrett is considered to be one of the best homicide men around."

"I'm not being critical of the methods used or the police department in anyway, but I believe my client is innocent."

"Then how did the victim's blood get on that whetstone?"

Lisa collected her thoughts and started to tell Chuck the entire scenario. "Freddie said Zaida was in the garden and had her finger stuck with a rose thorn. It bled profusely and he took a Kleenex from his pocket to stanch the blood. He then put the tissue back in his pocket to dispose of later. The whetstone was in the same pocket as the tissue.. That would explain how the blood got on the whetstone. What do you think?"

"Yes, I agree with you. How do you account for the time frame? He had access to the inside of the house until well after noon."

"Now Chuck, that's true, but a mitigating factor concerning the time frame was the fact my client said when he left, the victim was arranging the roses he's picked. When the murder was reported, the roses were still not completely arranged. Wouldn't that lead you to believe more time transpired than was accounted for when 911 was called?"

"That's a good point. You know the house guest said when he and Susan were leaving for lunch, Zaida and Freddie were walking toward the back door. He was carrying the basket of roses. They couldn't tell exactly what time they returned, but Freddie had already left for the day."

"Chuck, these are just two things that cause me to think my client isn't guilty without a reasonable doubt."

Chuck knew the position of the victim at the time of death was not what it should have been physically, but he thought it best not to further clutter the field with anymore if's, and's, or but's.

Who Killed Zaida Moore?

The remaining dinner conversation was small talk about the practice of law and his recent move to the Tampa Bay Area.

"Lisa, this has been an enjoyable dinner. Perhaps we can do it again soon."

"Just give me a call," she said, "I promise I won't have to shampoo my hair or cuddle my pet cat."

"You're certain about that now?" Chuck said with a shake of his head and a smile. He had determined Lisa was a neat girl with a superb sense of humor.

They walked out and Chuck waited until Lisa had left her parking space to approach his car. He was behind her when they turned right onto Dale Mabry. She looked in the rearview mirror and caught his eye. An uplifted hand waved in a friendly manner to the first blind diner date the twenty-six year old attorney had been on in her life. On a scale of one to ten, she thought he would probably be an eight.

28

Since Chuck had met with Lisa, he was more convinced the wrong man was in jail. He had no idea, at the time, who the guilty party might be, but he didn't think it was Freddie. He just didn't fit the mold of a murderer according to Chuck's idea of a suspect. He and Lisa finally were able to arrange a meeting with him at county jail. Even though there was a thick glass between them, they could communicate well.

"Freddie, the man with me is Chuck Wilson. He was hired to further investigate the Zaida Moore murder. Because he had a contract with the victim's father, he's still examining the case even though you've been charged. Will you speak with us?"

Freddie looked at the stranger and answered Lisa. "Yes, I'll be glad to talk to you. Miz Swanson, you know I had nothing to do with Miz Moore's murder. I would never do a thing like that," Freddie pleaded.

"Now Freddie, the evidence points to you, even though we both know it's circumstantial. Now I want you to think back to the day of the murder. Remember when you two were walking to the back door, Mark and Susan, who were staying in the guest house, were driving down the driveway going to lunch."

"Yes, I remember that. They waved to us as they left."

"How long were you in the kitchen?"

Who Killed Zaida Moore?

"It couldn't have been more than twenty minutes. I've had lots of time to think since I been here. When I was on my way home, I stopped to buy a little gas and a pack of cigarettes. The store is a convenience store on Nebraska near Palm. I been there before to buy gas, cigarettes and a candy bar, but I don't know if anyone would know me."

"Freddie, it may be worth a try to see. I'm going to get a photograph of you and take it by the store. I'll call Grace to have it ready and Chuck and I will swing by to pick it up."

"Chuck, do you think you can do me any good?" a worried Freddie asked.

"Man, I don't know and I'm not giving you any false hope, but I'll do what I can."

"Some people are talking about the lectric chair. You know that can happen."

Chuck had to admit some people who were innocent had been executed but advised Freddie not to dwell on the possibility since he had such a good attorney.

When Chuck and Lisa were leaving the visiting area, Freddie was being taken back to his cell. Lisa took out her cell phone and called Grace. She told her to have a good, recent picture of Freddie ready and they would swing by and pick it up. They were at the apartment within ten minutes. Grace met them at the door with the picture. Lisa determined he was about five years younger, but it was a good likeness to help with the identification.

The convenience store was close by, so Chuck and Lisa decided to stop there before they headed to their homes on the far side of town. A clerk was behind the counter taking cash for a gas sale. Lisa asked if she could speak to him briefly. He called the owner from the back of the store. He came out and the three huddled in the corner by the drink case for privacy.

"Sir, would you recognize one of your customers if you were shown a photograph of him?" Lisa inquired.

"I may, but I have over six hundred customers coming through the door daily."

"He said he stopped by here often to get cigarettes and gas."

"Let me see the snapshot," the man said.

Lisa said, "Before you look at it, he is five years older. Now, he has a mustache and shorter hair."

"I know him. He is a guy named Barnes. I remember him because he borrowed a gas can from me. He had run out of gas about half mile down the street. Also, I cashed a check for him before. He's a nice fellow."

"Did you see him about four weeks ago? It would have been on a Friday."

"No, I couldn't say he came in at a certain time. Usually I'm in the back taking care of deliveries and orders. I'm sorry"

"Well, so much for that," Chuck said as the two walked to his car.

"I'm still sure he was not involved in any way. I don't think he was near the Moore home when the crime occurred," Lisa said.

"Lisa, would you join me for lunch. I found a little restaurant that makes delicious Cuban sandwiches. We can slip in and out quickly. I'm busy and I know you are too."

"I can spare a little time. We do have to stop for lunch even if we are busy."

"It's right down from my apartment off Dale Mabry."

Since it was almost 2:00 p.m., the restaurant was nearly empty. Lisa and Chuck found a vacant booth and sat down. Their order was taken by the owner who went into the kitchen to prepare two sandwiches served with chips and a coke.

"Now Chuck, what do you think after you've met Freddie Barnes?"

Chuck didn't answer. Lisa thought he hadn't heard the question. "Well?"

"I heard you. I was rolling the question around in my gray orb. Now, here's what I think. I could be wrong, but I don't feel your client is guilty. If, as he says, he was in the house for twenty minutes, he couldn't have eaten, killed Zaida and left the scene and arrived home in less than forty five minutes. Did you ask his wife what time he came home?"

"She said she didn't look at the clock, but her soap opera was on. I checked the paper and it goes off at one thirty."

"Add the time up. He went into the house at about twelve-fifteen. Eating took twenty minutes. He said he lost no time leaving, and the drive took about twenty minutes. He stopped for gas, probably bought two or three dollars worth. He paid for it with cash. The transaction would have taken about ten minutes. Allow five minutes for parking and walking into his apartment. Giving him a little extra time, he arrived no later than one-ten. What time did you say the soap opera goes off?"

"It goes off at one-thirty. Actually, it goes off a little before then."

"You know Lisa, the time just doesn't add up."

"You're right. Also, I haven't been able to see him committing a murder and being so composed when he arrived home."

"Not that it matters, but are these two legal?"

"No, for obvious reasons, they haven't made it legal, but they've been together six years. To quote Freddie, they don't mess around in the street."

"When the case goes to trial, their status could affect the testimony. You know that's true."

"I've thought about that, and I don't think it'll be a problem."

"You say they're loyal to each other?"

"For six years."

"That's more than you can say for many legals out there."

"Come on Chuck, there are plenty out there who are loyal. You know that."

"I guess I just missed out."

"Chuck, how long were you married?"

"Four years, why do you ask?"

"Do you miss having someone in your life?"

"That's a long story. Maybe I'll tell you one of these days. Not now though."

"I appreciate what you have done to help me with Freddie's case. I don't want you to think I'm doing all this to gain notoriety. Actually, you know as well as I winning a high profile case like Zaida Moore's wouldn't hurt my future practice of law, but when I look at Freddie, I can't help but think prejudice. True, he was at the scene, but so were at least four other possible perps."

"How old did you say you are?" Chuck joked.

"You know I'm twenty six."

"You're pretty sharp for such a child, girl."

"Thanks for that back door compliment," Lisa answered.

"Anything else you need?" he asked.

"Not that I can think of."

"Lisa, I have to get home now. Got some work to do for Preston Spencer. I'll drop you off at your car. Next time, you can drive and I can view the scenery."

When Chuck pulled into the bank parking lot, he reached across the console and patted her hand. I'll call you soon."

Lisa looked at Chuck and slightly winked. She said, "I've just shampooed my hair and I don't even own a cat."

Who Killed Zaida Moore?

Chuck laughed, shook his head and departed.

Log: *Today we visited Freddie Barnes the African American accused of the murder of Zaida Moore. He could be guilty, but I don't think so at this time.*

Lisa is quite a gal. She has a good sense of humor and she is sharp. I felt the old excitement returning, even though I know it can't happen.
CWW

29

A sporty looking Moe Garrett arrived at the detective division the next morning.

He went into the office to see if any new cases had been assigned to him. A couple that he could probably clear with a phone call, or at most, a little conversation in person, were removed from his folder.

"Detective Garrett there's a gorgeous lady to see you. Is she your new girlfriend?" the clerk said as Moe peeked out the blind on the door.

"Listen Cathy, that lady sitting out there is Jean Hodges. She's a decent, hard working, single mother. She lives in public housing with her son. You know everyone isn't as lucky as you are. Don't make the mistake of underestimating her or being rude to her because she's not so attractive or well dressed."

The young, cute clerk typist had just been brought down a notch by one of the fairest, nicest men to ever don the blues of the Tampa Police Department. This fact she would never forget.

Detective Garrett walked out to the waiting room and shook the hand of Jean Hodges, "Why Ms. Hodges, it's good to see you, but what brings you here?"

"I don't know if it's important or not, but could we go somewhere and talk?"

Who Killed Zaida Moore?

"We can go into my office. Cathy, we are not to be disturbed."

"Yes sir, Detective Garrett."

Moe Garrett held his hand out to show Ms. Hodges into his office. She meekly sat in an offered chair. The homicide detective sat behind his desk facing her. Jean started to speak. "You do remember me don't you?"

"Of course I do, you were the Moores' housekeeper."

"I am the Moore's housekeeper. Mr. Moore called me last week and I started on Monday. I'm working this whole week to get caught up. Then, the house will be in good shape again. After that, I'll go on my regular days, Mondays and Thursdays."

"You know that was the saddest house I was ever in. It seemed that Mrs. Moore was everywhere. Her beautiful wedding picture hanging over the fireplace even seemed to have sad eyes. When I went into the kitchen, I couldn't help but cry. Mrs. Moore had a plastic bucket that she put roses in until she could arrange the bouquets for the hospital. That bucket still had roses in it. They were dead and the petals were in the water and on the floor. Those already put into the vase were dried up. I'm sure that Mr. Moore didn't even see those roses because he was so sad."

"Detective, have you ever been in that house? It's the most beautiful home that you have ever seen. The furniture is beautiful. The stairs and the banister is made out of some kind of wood that almost looks alive. It just gleams."

"I've been in the house once. I'll agree with you, it is a beautiful home.

"How's Mr. Moore holding up, Jean?"

"Oh, he seems pretty good sometimes. At other times, he seems lost and so sad."

"Okay, what's on your mind?"

Jean reached down and picked up a tote bag from beside the chair. She put it on her lap, stuck her hand into it, and pulled out a plastic baggie. She placed it before Detective Moe Garrett. "Yesterday, I pulled the couch out to vacuum under it. Stuck in the corner, behind the ruffle, was this piece of glass. I recognized it as a piece from a candy dish that Mrs. Moore kept on a coffee table. It's strange, but I missed that candy dish when I came back. It was her very favorite. She called it Lalique and told me that it was expensive and she would take care of it. I just figured that Mr. Moore had put it away since it reminded him of her. I picked up the piece of glass and noticed it had a little spot of brown on it. That's when I got to thinking it might be important. I went to the kitchen and got that plastic baggie and put it in it."

"Did you handle this piece of glass, Jean?" Detective Garrett asked as he turned the glass, enclosed in plastic, over and over..

"Yes, but I was wearing rubber gloves. I'm allergic to dust, mold and even some cleaning products, so I always wear them."

"I'll keep the glass here. I don't want to handle it too much. It may be more important than you think."

A big smile came across Jean's face as she said, "Detective Garrett, my tax refund came back and I bought me a car."

"That's great Jean, what did you get?"

"It's a Ford. It's ten years old, but my daddy said it's in good shape. If it gives any trouble, he said he most likely could fix it."

"I'm proud for you, Jean, you're sure to get ahead."

"Yes, sir. You know how long it takes to drive from the project to the Moore's home? Thirty-five minutes."

"I thank you so much for coming in. I'll be in touch." Garrett got up and opened the door to permit Jean Hodges to take leave. As he walked back into his office, he had the gut feeling that this small piece of glass might really upset the applecart. He didn't push any panic buttons yet, even though he couldn't help but be mesmerized by what he saw in the baggie on his desk.

Garrett didn't open the plastic bag, but took it straight to the lab. He left orders to have prints lifted. He told the lab tech not to touch the brown spot on the glass as it would be carefully analyzed later. Then he went to the records section. Since it was the lunch hour, Mr. Gonzalez was the only one checking files. Garrett asked him to check to see if Robert Earl Moore had ever been printed. As he searched, he said "Moore, Moore, Robert Earl. You're in luck, my friend. He worked at the country club when he was in college. Back then, if you worked where alcohol was served, you had to be fingerprinted. Take his Tampa Police Department number to ID and they'll help you."

Moe knew they wouldn't need to help him unless Moore's prints were on the piece of glass he'd left at the lab. As he was leaving, Roy Lopez, the lab tech, stopped him going out the door.

"Not so fast, Moe, I already have the prints lifted from that piece of glass. Easiest ones I ever lifted."

"How about a comparison, Roy."

"Let me get the P.D. number if one's available."

"Got it right here."

Roy pulled the print card of Robert Earl Moore. "By golly, they're identical. They're from a thumb and index finger. Now there's a little scar on the right index finger that wasn't there twenty years ago. If you want me to, I can check that spot for you. I won't damage it. We have chemicals that show if it's blood. Nothing really scientific, but I can also give you the blood type."

"Roy, you are the man of the hour. I'll wait in the cafeteria. I guess I can stand one more cup of Lazarra's pizon." Moe thought the war was won. He had it in the bag. Now, he wasn't so sure the whole case from beginning to end wasn't in the bag, the zip-lock bag a housekeeper so carefully brought to the police. Moe, being a product of the "no mistakes" school, was just a little concerned with the turn of events.

Roy was grinning when he strode into the cafeteria, "Got your info Garrett. It's type "AB positive." Anything else you need?"

"No, you've done all the damage you should do in one day, Roy. I thank you so much for all your help."

Garrett knew the piece of heavy crystal could have inflicted the fatal blow. As a matter of fact, it was more likely than a whetstone. The thing Garrett couldn't imagine, since he had no knowledge of Lalique, was the size and weight of the dish as it set on the table. He decided to go to the housing project one more time and talk to Jean Hodges. He hoped he could catch her at home. He knew she worked Mondays and Thurdays, but she was working all of this week to get the house back in shape. His watch read exactly 3:15 p.m. He knew Jean came home in time to pick up her little boy from school. He headed north. Twenty minutes later found him pulling into the projects where he had first interviewed Jean Hodges. He thought she lived in Court B, and he knew she would be driving a Ford. As luck would have it, Garrett pulled up just as Jean and her son were getting out of the car.

"This your son?"

"Yes, this is Jason. He's in second grade, going to be in third grade soon."

"I have to ask you about the candy dish, the one you brought the piece from."

"I'll help if I can, Detective Garrett."

"Fine, can you describe the dish?"

Who Killed Zaida Moore?

"Well, Mrs. Moore said it was Lalique. Mr. Moore gave it to her for her thirtieth birthday. It had fancy candy in it. She said it had a red bow tied to a beautiful diamond ring coming out of the top of the dish. The piece of crystal was so heavy, you had to lift it with both hands. It had a square bottom with a round top. Oh, there were several little birds around the dish part."

"Would you recognize a dish like it if you saw one?"

"I guess I would. I looked at that one for three years."

Garrett had called a local department store and was given the name of a jewelry store that carried Lalique. "Would it be possible for you and Jason to ride with me to Mathis Jewelry? They're located on this side of town so it shouldn't take long."

"Sure we can," she said, "Jason do you want to ride in this police car?"

"It's brown and it ain't got no red light or siren."

"Detective Garrett is a different kind of police officer than Officer Friendly that comes to your school." Jean buckled her son into the back seat, and got in beside Moe Garrett.

The drive to Mathis Jewelry took twenty minutes. Moe was certain this was Jean's first trip to the upscale store. As a matter of fact, it was his first and probably last visit, as a policeman's salary wouldn't support the taste that this store encouraged.

Moe got out and walked around and opened Jean's door for her. She got out and opened the back door and took Jason's hand and started into the store. As the three walked into the fancy store, a clerk met them and asked if she could help them?

"Yes," Moe answered. "We'd like to see the Lalique."

She kind of sniffed as she walked to a glass case and said rather curtly, "Any special piece?"

"May we just look?" Moe asked.

"Call me if you need my help," the clerk replied as she walked toward the back of the store.

"That's it right there. See the birds around it," Jean said as she pointed to the piece of Lalique.

"Miss, may we see that piece, please?" Garrett asked.

The clerk unlocked the glass case and placed the piece on a velvet square. Detective Garrett lifted the piece and exclaimed. "It's as heavy as lead. You could kill someone with that." As the clerk looked the other way, he winked at Jean and said, "Dear, are you sure this is the piece you want?"

Jean knew why he said it and played along with him, "I'm sure that's it."

They then left the store. Moe was grateful for Jean's help and commented on how well behaved Jason was.

He said, "I think a boy as nice as Jason should be rewarded." He pulled an envelope from his pocket and handed it to Jason.

He opened it and screamed, "Free passes to McDonalds! Thank you so much."

When he let them out of the car, he knew he had made a little boy happy. He hoped this would be his last trip to the public housing project, but he couldn't be sure, as the turn of events was rather disturbing.

30

Moe was extremely concerned about the piece of crystal found under the couch in the Moore living room. While he had no reason to suspect Bob, the evidence was there to support doubt. He decided to call Chuck Wilson to discuss if he had any further thoughts on the murder. The two decided to meet at the café where Moe and Hank, his friend and a fellow detective met. It was a quiet and convenient meeting place.

The two parked simultaneously and walked in together. Seats were taken at a back table. The two greeted each other with a handshake.

"How have you been, Chuck?"

"Busy since I last saw you," Chuck responded.

"Anything on the Moore case?"

"Not since I went to Freddie's neighborhood and talked to the manager of a convenience store where Freddie shops. Moe, I still don't think he's a murderer. I don't think Bob Moore thinks he did it."

"Chuck, something has developed since I last talked to you. It may be significant, or it may not be important at all."

"Can you tell me about it, or is it confidential?"

"We've shared information on this case before and I see no reason for secrecy now."

"I'm listening and believe me, you can trust me."

"Remember I told you the Moores had a housekeeper."

"Yes I know. The one who cleaned on Monday and Thursday."

"Right, Bob Moore called her back last Monday to resume her cleaning. She pulled the couch out to vacuum under it. In a corner, under the ruffle, she found a square piece of crystal. She knew immediately it was a piece from the candy dish off the cocktail table. I took her to a gift and jewelry store and she picked a piece exactly like the one that set on the table. I examined the bottom of the dish and it was square and about three inches wide. You know Doctor Sheppard said the murder weapon was about that size. There was a small brown spot on it which our tech identified as blood. You know whose **print** it is? Bob Moore's."

"You know both pieces of evidence could be explained. He may have touched the dish long before his wife's murder. That would account for the prints. The tiny spot of blood could have been cause by him sticking his finger without his knowing that he was bleeding."

"You're right. I've stuck my finger putting on my tie tack and TPD insignia. When you're warm and have been active, your blood does flow more freely."

"Moe, not that you would, but don't push any panic buttons yet."

"Oh no, but I do feel the need to evaluate completely the possibilities, since you too feel Freddie had nothing to do with the murder. He had positively nothing to gain and everything to lose."

"Moe, do you mind if I contact Lisa Swanson?"

"I can't see it would do any harm to tell her. Soft pedal it, don't dump it in her lap as a definite. Okay."

"I'd never do that. Two reasons. Number one, remember I was a policeman and still have the loyalty factor intact. Number two, lawyers are like doctors who want their patients to walk out healthy. The only difference is they want their clients to just walk."

"You're right on, Chuck."

"Don't think I don't respect Lisa and would help her within certain limits."

"I'm thinking of having a heart to heart with Jim Donavan. You know he's Bob Moore's best friend."

"Will he be totally objective, Moe?"

"I completely trust him," Moe assured Chuck.

"This restaurant reminds me of someone's hideaway."

"You're right. It's nice for meeting privately. The parking and entry being on the side, makes it easy to slip in and out without being seen from the main street."

"Think it was built like that on purpose?"

"Could've been. This was built for a pool hall or billiard parlor as they were called a while back."

"Anything else we need to discuss, Moe?" Chuck inquired.

"Not that I can think of. When you speak to Lisa, give her my regards," Moe said as the two crime stoppers walked to their cars.

Moe went to the records section and dictated a supplement to Robert Gonzalez. Chuck headed home to put the info into his computer while it was still hot in his head."

Log:
Log: *Today I met with Moe Garrett. There have been staggering developments in the Moore case.*
CWW

Chuck called Lisa at five thirty. She failed to answer her phone after several rings. He hung up, popped the top on a Coke and settled down to read the morning paper. After about thirty minutes, he tried again. She answered and he asked if she was busy. She told him she was a little late because she had stopped by the deli to pick up some sandwich fixings. Nothing was planned for the rest of the evening. They decided to meet at her apartment.

When Chuck arrived, Lisa had the wine cooling and two glasses waiting. She was at the door as soon as the doorbell rang. When she opened it, a smiling Chuck offered a small kiss, nothing sexy, just a brief connection from a handsome, kind and well intentioned male. Naturally, Lisa was just a little excited by the genuine show of affection.

"Nice place you have, girl," Chuck said as he glanced around the den.

"Oh, it'll do until I get established," Lisa responded. "Now, what brings you here on such short notice and out on a windy, rainy night? Not that I'm not glad to see you, but it has to be very important."

"It could be. Now don't get all hepped up over what I'm going to tell you. I met with Moe Garrett today."

"That Schmoo is so self-centered."

"Now Lisa, don't be so critical of Moe. I think, at least what I know of him, he is excellent in his investigative methods. While you two might not see eye to eye, under different circumstances, you could feel differently. Now, try to give Moe the benefit of the doubt. Incidentally, he sent you his regards."

"I'll try," Lisa said with venom in her voice. "Now let's get to the subject at hand."

"It seems that a heavy piece of crystal was found under the couch. While it could have been broken before or after the murder, it could have been the weapon. On the day of the funeral, the house was filled with people. It would have been easy for someone to have knocked the dish off the cocktail table."

"Wow!"

Chuck didn't mention the tiny spot of blood. He felt it would trigger a response from Freddie's attorney that could be detrimental to the entire investigation and possibly the trial also.

"Is wow your only comment?"

"You know how I've felt all along about Freddie's innocence," Lisa responded.

"Take my advice as a former police officer. Don't get too carried away about this, but keep it foremost on your list of possibilities."

"Chuck, I do appreciate you throwing a little cool water on me during my first baptism by fire."

"Did you say you had wine cooling?"

"Yes."

"Let's drink to our mutual admiration. Also, the fact you could have a winner in the trial of Freddie Eli Barnes."

"Chuck, I do admire you and would like to think you feel the same way about me. I don't mean as an attorney, I mean as a woman. You see my position, don't you?"

"Lisa, I find you very attractive and I do admire you. You know some things about me, but there are things that you're not aware of, and may never know."

"Such as?"

"I'll lay it out for you. When I was a security guard, I was shot in the lower abdomen and groin. It was pretty serious. The shot to my genitals left me with an injury that's called Peyronies acquired. What that means is a small section of my penis was damaged. The scar tissue causes it to take a strange turn. Now I've not had sex since it happened. I haven't really found a lady to whom I could tell this tale. The doctor said there was no reason for my celibacy as most women are built to handle the situation. Now, you know the reason for me trying not to get worked up over a gal that's sexy, attractive and bright."

The sexy, attractive and bright gal couldn't hold back the tears as she thought of what this man must have endured. "Let's have a glass of wine. Remember, you wanted to drink a toast to our mutual admiration."

"I didn't mean to sadden you, Lisa. My philosophy is we all have baggage. Mine just happens to be a little heavier that some people's."

"If I wanted, would you try to have sex with me?" The toast given, Chuck and Lisa enjoyed the cup and he said he had to get back to his apartment. He couldn't believe he had unloaded on her, but felt somewhat better knowing she hadn't rebuffed him. He purposely failed to acknowledge her question.

As he started to leave, she grabbed his face, held it, and kissed him. It was a lingering intimate kiss he felt was intended to remove any doubt that his damaged apparatus mattered. As he left, she walked him to the door. He turned, blew her a kiss and received one in return.

Who Killed Zaida Moore?

31

Moe was not a happy camper when he arrived at the detective division the next morning. He was over run with thought on the Zaida Moore murder. The night before, he had read and digested every word on the offense report. He still did not feel good about the whole investigation. He knew the crime scene technicians had done their job well. It did seem as though something was missing from the very first. They could only access what was present at the time. That left room for many variables. Finally, Moe decided to call Chuck to further enhance the total picture.

As it happened, Chuck was available when Moe called. The two decided to meet at a local park close to the downtown area. Moe only had a five minute drive so he arrived first. Since Chuck was unfamiliar with the area, Moe told him exactly how to get to the park with the least traffic. When he arrived, he had two large drinks. He took a seat across from Moe and put a drink in front of him.

"You're thoughtful, Chuck."

"No problem. Hope you like diet."

"You know Chuck, two heads are always better than one. I've been struggling with the whole picture of the Moore murder. When I went out to Bob's house, I didn't think he could have been the murderer. Now, I'm not sure. Your photos of the model left an impression on me. Also, your analysis of the door lock and layout of the residence added another dimension. Let me say, you earned an A for your investigative expertise."

"Moe, I try to think things through. Sometimes I get bogged down. You know I don't have a family, at least not with me. That makes a lot of difference."

"I think you were right on target when you determined the killer had to come in the back door. Let's think about how many people had access to the back entrance on the day of the crime."

"How many do you think, Moe?"

"We're talking about Bob Moore, Freddie Barnes, the two house guests and the exterminator. I don't think anyone else was there, do you?"

"I think that's it. You can eliminate the house guests and the exterminator. Who does that leave?" Chuck asked.

"Freddie and Bob," Moe agreed.

"You know I've interviewed both those parties, don't you?"

"Chuck, what was your honest feeling after talking to Freddie?"

"I could be wrong, but I had a gut feeling Freddie wasn't the guilty party. He had nothing to gain and everything to lose. Of greater importance was the time sequence."

"How so?"

"The day of the murder, Freddie said he was in the house eating a sandwich and drinking a Dr. Pepper. The victim was in the kitchen and had started to arrange the roses. All told, he said he was in the house not more than twenty minutes. That would be pushing him to eat, commit murder, stop to buy gas and still get home in less that an hour. The time has been substantiated by Grace. To check this out, I drove from the

Who Killed Zaida Moore?

Moore house to Freddie's apartment. I didn't break the speed limit and it took me over twenty minutes to drive the distance."

"Chuck, you know the evidence points to Freddie in every way. He was at the scene, her blood was on the murder weapon and he made a hasty getaway. These are all positives. There are really no negatives except for the reason for the crime. You know as well as I do there are often no whys in crimes of passion. Well, there probably are some, but the perp can't verbalize them."

"I agree with you, Moe. Now, there is one thing that hasn't been mentioned through the whole process. Not by the first officer on the scene, the coroner or even you."

"And, what might that be, sir?" Moe questioned as if referring to Sherlock Holmes.

"The approximate length of time the victim had been dead when the call was first made."

"Chuck, you know as well as I do, there's such a difference among cadavers that you can't tell for certain."

"But you could tell if the body had been lifeless for almost two hours."

"Well yes, by that time rigor mortis has usually set in. Now you know, that also can vary according to the health and stamina of the victim," Moe recalled from his days as a criminal justice student.

"Did you tell me Zaida had small bruises on her upper arms?" Chuck asked.

"Yes, the pathologist never mentioned them, but the officer that originated the report did. Remember, at the time it was classified as an unexplained death."

"If Freddie left the house at twelve thirty and her husband found her at about two fifteen, that's a long time not to notice changes in the body of the deceased, don't you think, Moe?"

"Tell you what I'm going to do. I'm going to see Jim Donavan, Bob's best friend. He arrived at the Moore's just after the paramedics. He was a homicide detective for years. I'm certain he could tell us the state of the body when he first looked at it."

"Moe, have you considered the husband might have been the killer?"

"You know Chuck, I thought there was no way he could have been the murderer. Now I'll have to admit, there is a shadow of doubt in my mind. It's true, he is the grieving widower, but anyone can play the role. When I interviewed him at the station, he was totally devastated. He admitted at the time Zaida had a drinking problem, but he down played it. Since then, I've learned it was a real problem in many ways. That's no reason to kill your wife, is it?"

"Did the autopsy mention blood alcohol content?" Chuck asked.

"It wasn't recorded, but I know for a fact Zaida was nearly drunk on the day of her death."

"You know Moe, the plot is thickening, isn't it?" said Chuck.

"Yes, Chuck. I am grateful for your input in this homicide investigation. I know no favoritism has been shown to these well knowns, but you, being from out of town, have a different slant on the 'who's the most likely guilty party?' than maybe a local."

"I've taken it on its face value. I know no one except Preston Spencer, and his secretary."

"Chuck, when I've spoken to Captain Donavan, I'll give you a call and let you know his take on the situation."

"I have my cell phone with me at all times. I'll be waiting to hear from you. See you, man," Chuck said as the two walked to their cars.

Who Killed Zaida Moore?

Moe stopped for a bite of lunch and checked back in to the detective division at nearly one o'clock. He went to communications and was met by Jim Donavan who had just returned from lunch. The two went to the cafeteria and chose a table far back in the restaurant.

"What's on your mind, Moe?"

"I'll tell you Jim, the Zaida Moore murder has gotten more frustrating each day. You know the investigator Zaida's father hired has brought up many points that have to be reckoned with. Now, I'm going to have to say the case is as full of holes as a colander. That's what brings me here to talk to you."

Donavan puffed on his cigar and blew a cloud of smoke as he said, "Shoot."

"You know you were one of the first people at the crime scene. Can you tell how long you thought the victim had been dead when you looked at her?"

"Okay., here goes. First off, I was not there as an officer of the law, I was there as a friend of the victim's husband. You can see how this might affect my observation, can't you?"

"Yes, I understand exactly what you mean."

"Moe, listen to me carefully. When I entered the front door, I looked at the corpse lying on the floor. Her coloring was a bluish-gray. There was no evidence of postmortem lividity. Her body showed no signs of rigor mortis having been started. As you know, postmortem lividity can start within twenty minutes after death. I thought at the time, she could have been placed there or fallen down the stairs just before our arrival. Moe, you know how a person will turn blue when they are choking? That's almost the coloring Zaida had with just a bit more paleness. Now, if rigor mortis had already set in, you could say the death occurred about two hours before our arrival."

"Jim, I'm certain you know what you're saying will shed new light on the case. Are you sure you remember the entire scene as it was?"

" Remember, you're talking to a seven year detective, much of the time which was spent in homicide."

"I'm aware of that. Now, could Bob have misrepresented the time frame on the day of the death?"

"He could have. You know anything is possible when you are as upset as Bob was that day, but still I don't think he's connected to the murder."

"There's almost a two hour time lapse from the time Freddie left the Moore home and the call to 911."

"Don't jump to conclusions, Moe. There's probably a reasonable explanation for all questions that have been raised."

"Thanks Jim, for your help in this matter. As we've said before, don't tell a soul about our conversation."

"Got you Moe. See you later."

The two men left the cafeteria. Jim went back to communications to supervise his personnel. Moe went upstairs to the detective division to place a call to Chuck Wilson.

32

A week had passed since Chuck and Lisa had interviewed Freddie at County Jail. Chuck felt something was missing from his investigation. He had assured Preston Spencer he would reveal the killer. So far, he was unsure if the perp was incarcerated or enjoying life each day her parents missed their beloved daughter. He finally made the decision to do a sweep of Freddie's neighborhood. He knew tongues sometimes wagged and revealed valuable unmentioned facts.

 Chuck had been to the neighborhood to pick up the photos to show the store manager. He knew he could find the complex even though the east side of town was foreign to him.

 He didn't want to stand out like a rat on a banquet table, so he carefully dressed in loose fitting pants, a large tee shirt and well worn sneakers. He pulled a ball cap down low over his forehead to cover his hair.

 His drive to the complex was uneventful. He parked the car and started to walk toward what he thought was Freddie's apartment. He noticed two elderly men playing checkers. "Can I disturb you for a minute?" he asked.

 Both men looked up, but said nothing. Finally, after looking Chuck over completely one said, "What you want?"

Chuck said, "I'm a private investigator. Here's my identification."

The man who had acknowledged Chuck said, "We ain't talking to no policeman."

"I'm not a policeman. I am a private investigator. I'm trying to help one of your friends who's been charged with murder."

"Do you be talking about Little Man Barnes?" the man asked.

"Would he also be called Freddie Barnes?" Chuck inquired.

"Yeah, that his name. He been charged with murdering the lady he work for."

"I'm not so sure he did the crime," Chuck advised. "Do you two know Freddie Barnes well?"

"I guess we do. He some kin to me. Not much, but I know'd him all his life."

The other checker player decided to add his comment to the discussion. "We both know him. We play checkers here every day. Our friends come and stand round and make bets on the side on who will win the game. When they leave, if they've won, they'll throw a little money our way. Sometimes we have ten standing round. It lotsa fun."

"Okay, I want you two to tell me if you saw Freddie the day Mrs. Moore was murdered. I'm sure the word got around about the murder."

"Oh yeah, we heard. Freddie stopped by that day. He said he couldn't stay cause he had to take Grace to buy groceries."

"Would you know about what time it was?" Chuck asked.

"Not exactly, but it was after lunch. I had done eat my lunch and watched the weather on television. I'm saying it was probably just before one o'clock."

"Did you see him leave that day?" Chuck asked.

Who Killed Zaida Moore?

"Yeah, he done changed his clothes when he came out. Him, Grace and the baby got in the car and left."

"Tell me, what kind of person is Freddie Barnes?" Chuck asked the two men.

"This what I think. Freddie is one nice man. He stay home with his family. He don't mess with the low lifes in the street. I ain't seen him with any these drug dealers either," checker player said.

"You right," the other checker player agreed.

Nothing else was said. Chuck backed up and the checker game proceeded. He watched for a few minutes, amazed at the level of play these two exhibited. No wonder they drew a crowd. He had to leave, so he thanked the two for their help.

"Mister, help our brother if you can. He ain't done no murder."

Chuck also felt that he hadn't committed a murder, but proving it was something else. He decided he would call Lisa to report on his encounter with the friends of Freddie Barnes.

He arrived home, sat down at the computer and made an entry into his log.

Log: *Today I spoke to two of Freddie Barnes friends. They substantiated the time Freddie said he returned home. I'm convinced Freddie Eli Barnes did not kill Zaida Moore. Who did?*

CWW

Chuck punched Lisa's phome number. She answered on the third ring.

"Lisa, this is Chuck. Are you busy?"

"No, I just arrived home a few minutes ago."

"Do you have plans for tonight?" Chuck asked.

"No, actually I was going to catch up on some correspondence. What did you have in mind?"

"Remember, I told you I made a mean salad. I can throw one together for the two of us. I need to talk to you about something that's developed."

"What time would you want me there?"

Chuck replied, "You can come anytime. It'll take me about thirty minutes to make the salad."

"Why don't I plan to come at six forty five."

"That'll be good. Do you know in which apartment complex I live?"

"I do, but what is your number?"

"It's fourteen. As you come in, it's the second building. It's marked B on the side. Think you can find it? If not, I could meet you out front."

"I'll be okay. You don't need to wait outside."

Chuck was waiting when Lisa arrived at the door. He took her arm and walked her into the living room. "Now Lisa, I don't want you to be impressed with all my finery. You know, some of us have it and some don't."

Lisa looked around and in a sweet voice said, "It's really neat."

Chuck's response, "It's early Goodwill. It does serve the purpose. The only thing new is the bedding. Well girl, did you bring a bunny appetite? It's ready."

"Where do you want me to sit, Chuck?"

Chuck pulled out a chair and said, "A special chair for a special lady."

When he pushed the chair in, Lisa had a warm glow. She didn't want it to show since they had the discussion about their relationship. She commented on the salad and the crackers which Chuck had served on an attractive glass plate.

"Would you like a glass of wine? It's not pricey, but it's good."

"That sounds good."

Who Killed Zaida Moore?

Chuck removed a bottle of white wine from the fridge and poured two glasses for them. He remarked that the stemware was also a Goodwill purchase."

The salad did in fact show he was a creative chef. He was pleased when Lisa complimented him on his culinary ability.

"I told you I could make a salad," he said.

"You know Chuck, sometimes it's not what's cooked, but the way it's served. The expression of caring that's evident."

"I never thought of it that way, but you do have a point."

Lisa responded, "I can't cook very much, but I can make a mean hot dog."

"Will you favor me with one some day?" Chuck asked.

"Consider it on the agenda. Your choice of time and place."

"Lisa, you didn't know I went back to Freddie's neighborhood. I spoke with two men who knew him. One claimed to be kin to him."

"After the encounter, what did you think?" the interested defense attorney inquired.

"I'm convinced Freddie had nothing to do with the murder. I don't know who's responsible, but I think I know who's not."

"What do you base your decision on?" Lisa asked.

"Actually the two men said positively that Freddie was home long before the report says the victim was discovered by the husband. One man said Freddie, Grace and the baby left shortly after he came home. Both men had known him for his entire life and they stated he was a very good man and responsible father and mate to Grace. Now think, why would Freddie kill his source of income? What did he stand to gain?"

"As I've said before, Freddie denies any knowledge of the crime," Lisa agreed with Chuck.

"Chuck, when you were a police officer did you investigate a murder?"

"Several."

"You would know how long a person had been dead by the condition of the corpse, wouldn't you?"

"Generally, as a matter of fact, all policemen read and study all phases of decomposition of the human body from the last breath to the skeletal remains. It may be gross, but this is how many murders are solved. The old saying is 'check the W's.' What that means is the why, where, when, who, and what."

"You enjoyed the profession, didn't you?"

"Oh yes. Lisa, let's shift gears. I don't think I told you, but I think your outfit is pretty hot."

"I'm glad you noticed."

"I'd have had to be blind not to have noticed."

"It's about time for me to leave for home."

As Lisa got up from the table, Chuck put his arm around her shoulder. She turned her face to him. He kissed her on the cheek. She offered her face uplifted to his. "I'm sorry Lisa. It can't happen. I'd give anything if it could, but it's just not possible."

"Is there something wrong with me?"

"Oh no Lisa. You are some sexy gal, more appealing than you know. Also I've realized I'm physically attracted to you, your voice, your looks, your figure, even the way you smell. I love your sense of humor and your realistic approach to life. You're precious."

"Thanks for all your help in the case. I know Freddie appreciates it too."

"Now remember, I'm still on Preston Spencer's payroll. We signed a contract for at least a month."

"That's right. I seem to forget that.".

Who Killed Zaida Moore?

Chuck followed Lisa to the door. He raised her hand and kissed it. She responded by pressing his hand between hers.

"Lisa, thanks for coming."

"I wouldn't have missed it for the world."

33

When Chuck awakened the next morning, he had a change in his attitude. He felt his old persona returning and wondered if his visit with Lisa the night before was the reason for his overwhelming peace of mind. He buried his head in his pillow and actually thought he smelled her perfume. What the hell has gotten into me, he thought. I have things to do and people to see. With that, he bailed out of bed and hit the shower.

The first person he planned to call on was Preston Spencer. Even though there was a suspect in the county jail, he wanted to bring up a few questions that concerned him. He continued to have some serious doubts about Freddie's guilt. He parked his car and walked into the office.

"Mrs. Troxley, how are you today?"

"Chuck, when you reach a certain age, you don't have any good days, you just have some that are worse than others. Today isn't so bad. I actually caught myself singing on the way to work this morning."

"Great. Is Mr. Spencer in?"

"Yes, just go on into his office. He doesn't have an appointment until ten o'clock."

Who Killed Zaida Moore?

Chuck tapped softly on the door and was invited in by Preston Spencer. "Well, my man, it's good to see you. Join me in a cup of coffee. It's fresh. Mildred just made it."

"She still makes your coffee?"

"Oh yes, she's from the old school," Preston answered.

"I thought I would stop by to give you an update on the investigation."

"Good, and you can pick up your check. It's on Mildred's desk."

"You know I feel guilty getting paid when there's a man sitting in county jail."

"Now Chuck, a contract is a contract. Don't mention it again."

"There are a couple of things I would like to discuss with you, but first, how is Mrs. Spencer?"

"She seems to be a little better. Yesterday I took her shopping. She shopped for a few things. I felt her desire to get out was a definite improvement. She actually smiled at the cashier."

"Great, here's what I want to speak to you about. Freddie's defense attorney is certain her client is innocent."

"If she felt any differently, she wouldn't be much of an attorney, would she?"

"You're right. Now, I have my doubts about his guilt also. To summarize it, the time sequence and the reason, does not add up. Not only that, but Freddie's never had much of a criminal history. He swears he did not harm your daughter. To put it succinctly, I, too think he's innocent."

"If you don't mind, can I ask you a few questions about Zaida and Bob's relationship?"

"Sure. I don't think it would create a problem."

"How did they get along?"

"You know Chuck, theirs was a very complex marriage. I'm sure Zaida loved Bob, but it seemed to be based on money. There's nothing wrong with being concerned with your finances, but being possessed with it can destroy even the best of marriages."

"Did they disagree over her spending?" Chuck asked.

"Not in front of me, but she complained to her mother that he was tight. I don't see how he could be a scrooge with their lifestyle, but that's what she said," Preston related as he shook his head.

"Did he buy her expensive gifts?" Chuck questioned.

"Yes, he never forgot her birthday or anniversary. At Christmas, he really went all out."

"Were you and her mother at their home shortly before she was found dead?"

"Yes, we were there two days before her death. Her mother was entertaining her bridge club and Zaida fixed a beautiful bouquet of roses for her. You know she loved roses," Preston sadly replied.

"Did you go into the living room when you were there?"

"We did, Preston answered. "Her mother liked a certain candy Zaida bought. We went into the room and her mother took a couple of pieces from the dish on the cocktail table."

"What kind of candy dish was it, if you can recall?"

"It's a beautiful candy dish with birds on it."

"Do you remember seeing the dish when the family was there after the tragedy?" Chuck inquired.

"I really can't say. We were all so completely devastated. I can't recall anything. You might ask Bob if it's important."

"No it's all right. I just thought I'd ask you."

"Is there anything else you want to know?" Preston asked as he pulled a folder from his desk drawer.

"Not at this time, but if there is, I'll make a note and mention it at our next meeting."

Chuck could read the signs and knew it was time to depart. He thanked Mildred Troxley as she handed him his check. He left the office and headed back to his apartment.

Chuck reflected on the conversation he'd had with Preston Spencer. He wondered how one could be considered tight when he lived in a multi-million dollar home. Oh well, he thought, tight comes at different levels for different people.

D.E.Joyner

34

Chuck couldn't get Lisa out of his mind since the night before. He decided to ask her out to dinner if she had no plans for the evening. He really wanted it to be a special occasion so he stopped at a florist and bought a small bouquet of daisies. He thought they were simply elegant with a pale green bow in front.

When he entered his apartment, he put his info into the computer. He entered the check into his bookkeeping system. All done, he left to have lunch at a neighborhood diner. He looked at his watch several times and thought time wasn't moving very quickly. After a leisurely lunch, he went home, read a complete Playboy magazine and did his week's ironing. When five thirty came, he called Lisa. He breathed a sigh of relief when she answered quicky.

"Have a good day?" he asked.

"I've had better, but it was all right."

"Do you have plans for dinner?"

"Not really. What did you have in mind?"

"How about if I pick you up at say six-thirty," Chuck said.

"That'll work. All I have to do is change into something more casual."

"Now don't overdo it. We're not going clubbing, we're just going out to dinner."

"I'll be waiting," she answered.

When Lisa answered the door, there stood Chuck with a bouquet of daisies. "They're beautiful Chuck. How did you know daisies are my favorite flower.?"

"I didn't, but I thought they had an elegant beauty that matched yours."

"These are the first flowers I've received since my senior prom," she said, placing them on an end table. "Now, can I thank you properly?"

"Go for it," Chuck said holding his arms by his side.

"Lisa grabbed Chuck around his waist and kissed him passionately. He put his arms around her and pulled her tightly to him. He returned her kiss.

"Enough of this, we'll have plenty of time after dinner he said.

"Chuck, what would you like for dinner?"

"It's your choice. I really don't care."

"Is Italian all right? There's a good Italian restaurant close by."

"Sounds good, but you'll have to tell me how to get there." Chuck said, backing out of the parking place.

"It's only about three blocks down on your right."

Chuck pulled into the parking lot, got out of the car, and walked around to help Lisa from the car. The two walked into the restaurant and were seated immediately. A candle flickered between them creating a perfect atmosphere.

Dinner was enjoyed without one word about the Moore murder. Instead, they talked about their families. Lisa had wanted to ask about Chuck's son, but didn't want to seem prying. He seemed to want to talk about him, his school and his activities.

Dinner over, the two returned to Lisa's apartment. Instead of taking two chairs, as they usually did, they shared a corner of the couch.

"Lisa, I've thought about you all day."

"That's weird, I've thought about you too."

"We do have to be realistic about things. I'm not, and haven't been involved with anyone since the accident." As he spoke, he pulled her close to him.

"I've had serious relationships, but I haven't been in one for some time now."

"How do you really feel about me, Lisa"

"You're sure you really want to know? I think you're handsome, bright, and very sexy. Want me to go on?"

"No, you're embarrassing me with all those superlatives," Chuck answered.

"Not intended," she responded.

Chuck excused himself and headed toward the bathroom. When he was gone for several minutes, Lisa became concerned. She could see the bathroom was empty, and walked into the bedroom. There, Chuck was sitting on the bed. He had his shirt unbuttoned and his belt unfastened.

"Is something the matter, Chuck?"

"Nothing that hasn't been the matter for the past few years. Lisa, I don't want to embarrass you, but you really should know what I was telling you about the injury." Chuck stood up and exposed his damaged manhood. "This is what it's all about. You asked if I would try to have sex if you wanted. I think you know the answer, don't you?"

Lisa started to remove her blouse. Her unzipped slacks fell to the floor along with bra and panties. She was in bed with Chuck beside her, instantly.

As she rested on his shoulder, winding his chest hair around her index finger, Chuck said, "Well, how was it?"

"All I can say is every man needs to have an acquired Peyronies."

"That good, huh?"

"Better than good," she sighed as Chuck pulled her close and kissed her.

35

Arrests for Murder One are not usually mistakes. Generally the suspect is known by the victim. Many murders are solved almost before the victim gets cold, surely before rigor mortis sets in. All along, Moe had a premonition that something was amiss in the Zaida Moore case. He had his negative vibes reinforced by finding the broken piece of crystal. Could the killer have been Mark Pierce, who was surprised while he was stealing Zaida's pricey jewelry? Could it have been someone from the outside who came to service an appliance? Lastly, even though Moe didn't think so, could it have been Bob Moore? All of these possibilities were zooming around in Moe Garrett's head. The only thing he was sure of was that the blood on the crystal didn't belong to Zaida, whose blood type was certified by records to be "A negative."

Moe had misgivings from the beginning about the arrest of Freddie Barnes. Now, he was more confused by the blood on the crystal.

Finally, Moe decided to talk to Captain Donavan. He laid out his misgivings about the crystal piece with the "AB positive" blood on it. The Captain stopped him. "Wait, Moe, did you say it had a smear of "AB positive" blood on it?"

"Yes, Jim, that's what I said."

Who Killed Zaida Moore?

"I don't want to throw up a red flag, but I believe, in fact I'm sure that Bob's blood type is "AB positive." The reason I'm so certain is when Zaida became pregnant, there was a lot of talk about the Rh negative and positive factors not being compatible. This just might be a coincidence, however I think that "AB positive" is rare.

Captain Donavan finally decided the case had both negatives and positives for Bob Moore and Freddie Barnes. He determined the arrest of Freddie carried more weight. To be fair, he said he would go see his best friend and straighten some things out. He mainly wanted to know how a piece of broken crystal was found under the couch by the housekeeper.

Bob called the garage and had a patrol car brought to the back door. He headed out Bayshore Boulevard. No beauty was observed as he winded his way toward Bob's lovely home.

He was met at the door by Bob, who was obviously very depressed. Bob invited his friend in with a hug.

"Bob, something new had turned up in Zaida's murder investigation."

"What's that, Jim?"

"A large piece of broken crystal was found under the couch by your housekeeper. It had your identified fingerprints on it. Also, the blood found on it was "AB positive." Can you explain this?"

"I probably can, but, Jim, will you try to understand what I feel?"

"I'm listening and believe me, I'll try to understand."

"You know the Friday she died I came home early, just after two o'clock. I thought that Mark, Susan, Zaida and I could go for an early dinner and then take the boat out for a moonlight cruise. Zaida was in the kitchen arranging roses at the utility sink. She was almost drunk. The only thing I said was, "Oh no, not again." She flew into me and started cursing and calling me all kinds of names. I told her I was tired of the demeaning, the drinking, and the abuse I had to put up with. I walked from the kitchen and sat down to watch television. She followed me into the family room, calling me more names. I got up and went into the living room to get away from her. She followed me, cursing and screaming. I jumped up and grabbed her by her upper arms. I asked her if a divorce was what she wanted. She said I could have a fucking divorce, but she'd get half of my net worth.

I can't explain why I did what I did next. It just happened. I pushed her onto the couch. She fell on her side. I grabbed the candy dish and struck her on the back of the head. The candy dish slipped from my hand, hit the floor and broke. Pieces went all over the floor. Believe me, Jim, I didn't mean to kill Zaida. I think my anger and frustration got out of control. Actually, the blow wasn't very hard. There was very little blood, but her body stiffened and she stopped breathing. I got a small cut on my index finger that bled worse than her head. Within a minute, Zaida had turned bluish-gray. I knew something was bad wrong."

"Then, I grabbed her from the couch and pulled her over to the foot of the stairs. I cleaned up the broken glass and put the pieces in the trash compacter. When I finished, I called you. You know the rest."

"Bob, do you realize that your gardener, Freddie Barnes, is sitting in county jail being charged with Murder One?"

"I didn't want any of this to happen. It's been like a nightmare. Can you help get Freddie out?"

"Of course he'll get out, since he had nothing to do with the murder."

"Jim, we've always been friends," blubbered Bob. "Please tell me this won't change our relationship."

"It won't, but you know you'll be arrested within the hour."

"Can I have a little private time?" I want to call my mother and dad."

Who Killed Zaida Moore?

"Yes, let me call Detective Garrett. I'll stay with you 'till he gets here to make the arrest."

As Jim Dialed Moe's number from the kitchen phone, he observed Bob go from the house to the storage shed. As he spoke to Moe, there was a loud blast from the back yard. He said, "Moe, get here quick. I don't what that noise was, but I think it was a gunshot."

Jim hung up the phone and walked toward the direction from which the sound came. Gunsmoke and smell of gunpowder permeated the air. It was coming from an opening in the shed door. Jim cracked the door a little more and saw Bob's body lying partially draped over the work bench. The horrid scene left no doubt that his friend was dead.

A distraught Jim Donavan cried openly. His distorted face was a mirror of sadness. His only comment, said through sobs was, "I'll never understand the things people do in a fit of rage."

Jim looked at the door handle and noticed a small index card pushed through the opening. He pulled it out and read the contents.

To Jim,
       I'm sorry. Love you man.
Bob

To some policeman the words 'I'm sorry' meant, 'I'm sorry I got caught.' To Jim, these words from a friend for over twenty years meant I'm sorry I let you down. Will you remember the good times always?

36

The next morning Moe Garrett, Inspector Bridges and Lisa Swanson were at the county jail before eight o'clock. They were there to affect Freddie's release. When Freddie walked into the waiting area, he was all smiles. His jail-issued clothing had been replaced by jeans and a nice knit shirt. His feet didn't have flip flops, but he was wearing Nikes. The first thing he said was, "Where's Grace and Carinda?"

"They're waiting for you in your car," Lisa Swanson said.

"I sure want to see my baby and her mama. Then, I want to stop for breakfast and have bacon and eggs. I don't ever want to see another bologna sandwich." Freddie started to his car, but was stopped by Detective Moe Garrett. "Not so fast man. Call me tomorrow morning. I may have some more good news for you."

When Moe Garrett got back to the police station, he placed a call to a friend who was a supervisor at the water department. When he answered his phone, Moe asked if he could use a good, responsible employee. "No, I don't think he has much of a criminal record." Moe answered the question always asked.

When Freddie Barnes called the next morning, Moe gave him the good news. He told him to go to City Hall and give them his name and they would do the rest. Moe told him the next time he cared for any roses, they would be his own, in his own yard.

D.E.Joyner

37

It had been three months since the Moore murder had commanded the attention of the police department and the mass media. Moe Garrett was relieved that the whole scenario was behind him. He didn't feel that it was his brightest moment as a detective. With his mind free and the summer almost over, he met his friend Jim Donovan in the cafeteria. Jim had his usual stogie fired up and a cup of coffee in hand. "Moe, come on back here and let's catch up on things."

"Will Jim, what have you been doing?" Moe inquired.

"Well, we went to D.C. We felt that the kids are old enough to appreciate their heritage and the history of their country."

"Great trip?" asked Moe.

"Well, Moe, how great can a trip be when four kids are vying for space in a four door sedan? Really, they did have a wonderful time. They played games every time they were in the car. You know they played the same car games that we played when we were cooped up in the car. Remember Punch Buggy and Riddle Me, Riddle Me Roddle Me Ree? When they started that one, I wanted to join in. Dot said to keep my eyes on the road."

Who Killed Zaida Moore?

"Your vacation sounds great."

"It was. We took some good shots of important landmarks. If you, Lou Ann, and Mary Beth come over, I'll make some killer hamburgers on the grill and we'll look at the slides. Now, what did you two do on your vacation?"

"We went on a motorcycle tour of the Southwest. Lou Ann's mother and father just moved into our house and cared for Mary Beth. They felt that it would be less stressful if she were at her own home with her fenced yard.

"How long were you two gone?"

"Almost two weeks. We were both anxious to get home and see our gal. We missed her even though we called every day to check on things."

"Moe, let's change gears. You know we've not talked since Bob Moore's suicide."

"Captain, it's not something I like to think about, but the thoughts creep into my mind before I know it."

"He was my best friend for over twenty years," said Donavan. "I feel that I let him down by not being there for him when he needed me. I've read that friends and family always feel guilt when a loved one commits suicide."

"I've heard that too, Jim. I've often thought that when a person is determined to take their life, they will eventually do it no matter what. Most people would be content to have Bob Moore's possessions, which just goes to show that money alone won't buy happiness. Don't you agree?"

"Absolutely, I'm wondering where the money is going to come from when it's time for college. But I'm still a happy, contented man."

"That makes two of us."

"Moe, what are you hearing about the sergeant's test?"

"Not much, no news is good news, right?"

"It'll happen. The fiscal year has just started. As a rule, promotions and raises are included in the new yearly budget. I'll bet your name is at the very top of the list."

"Maybe not at the top, but at least on it."

"I've got a meeting, I'll see you later. Tell Lou Ann hello for me."

"See you, Captain," Moe responded as Jim left the cafeteria headed to the radio room.

Within the month, a list of those officers who had made sergeant was formally announced. It came as no surprise that Morris Daniel Garrett was one of those promoted. Also on the list was a veteran detective, Henry Lamar Crandell, who had an outstanding career in law enforcement and was now a sergeant.

The two remained in the detective division temporarily, but they knew that would change. To celebrate the promotions, the two friends, their wives, and Inspector Bridges and his wife, were treated to an evening out at one of Tampa's premier restaurants. The two honorees made toasts. Sergeant Hank Crandell stood and looked at everyone at the table. "Sometimes our chosen career isn't easy. You can expect some bad days and nights along the way. Then a night like tonight occurs and you're made aware of all your many blessings. I thank you and I love you guys."

Sergeant Moe Garrett knew he was next. He stood, his face beaming, "Hank, as usual, you're a hard act to follow, but I'll give it my best shot. When I chose law enforcement as a career, I soon found that the expectations were fiercely demanding. Our families too, have demands placed on them due to our absences. I want to thank all of you, especially Lou Ann.

This has to be the best job in the whole world. I can't think of anything I could do that would be more rewarding."

When he sat down, Hank's wife, Abbye and Moe's wife, Lou Ann got up and stood behind their husbands. They each pinned a tiny lapel pin on their husbands' jackets. The small, gold sergeants' stripes gleamed in the light. Both men kissed their wives who had sat beside them. The love and respect that their husbands showed them flowed throughout the room.

EPILOGUE

Moe Garrett:
He and Lou Ann still live in the same neighborhood. He continues to ride his Harley when he can find time. Lou Ann has given up riding due to having so many activities in which she and Mary Beth, who is a senior in high school, participate.

Captain Moe Garrett will soon retire with twenty-two years in law enforcement. He has served in every division. His last assignment was as a training instructor for new recruits. He is still considered a master homicide detective.

Chuck Wilson:
He remained a Tampa private investigator for four more years. An opportunity presented itself for him to purchase a polygraph practice. He is well known in the business of truth deception.

He and Lisa Swanson were married after a brief courtship. They are the proud parents of two young girls. Lisa Swanson Wilson has built a successful law practice in the Bay Area.

Who Killed Zaida Moore?

Chuck's wife remarried and decided to relinquish custody of their ten-year-old son to his father. He is now a second year cadet at West Point Military Academy.

Captain Jim Donavan:

He has been retired for several years. He and Dot had purchased a lake lot years ago. Their comfortable home is always filled with children and grandchildren. They all enjoy fishing, boating and just being together.

Their son, Jim Jr., is a law enforcement officer following in his father's footsteps.

Preston Spencer:

Unfortunately, he died within two years of Zaida's death. His death was attributed to a massive heart, but those who knew this kind, caring father, know he died of a broken heart. He could never accept Zaida's death at the hand of one who was supposed to love her.

His wife, who has dementia, has been confined to an assisted living facility for many years,

Freddie Eli Barnes:

He and Grace are still a loving couple. They now also have a son. Freddie still works for the Sanitation Department. He has held that good job with the city for many years. They have a beautiful yard with roses growing.

When they made their long, loyal relationship legal, Chuck and Lisa were present and offered heartfelt congratulations.

Jean Hodges:

She was able to move from the housing project. Her twenty-year-old son Jason went to a junior college, received an AA degree, and was recently accepted at the University of South

Florida. When he finishes college, he hopes to become a police officer. Naturally, his mother is extremely proud of her son.